The Spin

Elizabeth Kerr

Beirne Bridge Publishing
Charlottesville, VA

For Sally,
With fond memories
from Stuart Hall
Best wishes,
Lizzy

Beirne Bridge Publishing
PO Box 4643
Charlottesville, VA 22905

The Spin was first published in 2012 as Laundromat Girl

This book is a work of fiction. Names, characters, businesses, organizations, places, events and incidents are either the product to of the author's imagination or are used fictitiously. Any resemblance to actual persons, living or dead, events or locales are entire coincidental.

Cover by: Morgan Baxley
Interior design by Margie Baxley
Author Photo by Jennet Inglis

ISBN: 978-0-9980023-0-9

For Lucille Harris
who always said I had a book in me.

ACKNOWLEDGEMENTS

No book is born of a single person, certainly not this one. Janet Lembke deserves sainthood for her editing, moral support and firm foot on my behind. She dished out even portions of literary criticism and spicy homemade vegetable soup. She also supplied me with my favorite word in the narrative: "commando."

Special thanks go to Mari Selby and Jennet Inglis at Selbyink for patiently shepherding this book through the many legs of this journey to print. Books don't get there by themselves. They require careful nurturing and an occasional thwack.

The Spin was written over the course of twenty-two years and on a variety of versions of Microsoft Word. I am grateful to Mark Mones and Margie Baxley for formatting, and to Morgan Baxley for her cover design; without their assistance, this book would never see the light of day. James Scales at the University of Virginia provided the documentation I needed to anchor my story in reality. Thanks to Susan Shafarzak, Miles Fowler, Timmi Dillard, Pat Cheeks and my family for their support over the years. Thanks to Fred for his unwavering belief in my ability to tell a story. There are countless others who read drafts and sent me back to my keyboard to refine text or answer questions. Some just said, "Keep writing!" Thanks to you all.

"Write what you know" is a basic tenet in our craft. I have done just that. If you feel you have been represented in this work of fiction, I will take it as a compliment to my ability to recreate what I've experienced. All writers claim artistic license; we make the good people better and the bad ones worse, all in the name of good copy.

CHAPTER 1

Madeleine leaned forward, propped herself over her forearms on the counter, and surveyed her laundromat. Wisps of dust drifted across the tile floor amidst empty boxes of Tide and Rinso Blue. The trash bin was overflowing with empty Downy bottles and used softener sheets. At the base of the bin flies were giving last rites to the carcass of a Big Mac, recently fallen from its Styrofoam casket. She heaved a sigh and rolled around to face the drop-off area, her elbow never once lifting from the counter.

At thirty Madeleine was as married to her occupation as she was to the twenty-five extra pounds she gained after college. No amount of polishing her secretarial skills rewarded her with a new job, and no amount of dieting or exercise reduced her size 16 wardrobe. A Mae West body in a Twiggy-obsessed society, she comforted herself that no one would ever see *her* in a muumuu and slippers. Jeans and an oversized t-shirt were her standard issue, with red Nike rubber-toed sneakers at the foundation.

Pulling hot clothes from a dryer, she sorted the dry things, threw a few damp pieces back, and pondered men's underwear. Most men wore underwear, and those who went "commando" . . . well they didn't bear thinking about. On second thought, she did like the look. Her mind traveled on to styles of BVD's. There were those tight-fitting briefs and then there were boxer shorts. It seemed to her that rich college kids and professional types wore boxer shorts. It was more of a macho thing to wear briefs. She tried to imagine a Hell's Angel in boxers; no, they were the kind of guys who went commando. She shuddered to think of all the blisters they must have from riding with nothing but a seam between themselves and their bikes.

The current batch of laundry included six pairs of briefs, three of which were in tatters, the elastic stretching out several sizes, and a lone pair of boxer shorts.

"Now what do you suppose he uses these for?" Madeleine asked no one in particular. She held them up for inspection. There weren't many identifiable stains, nothing indicating heavy outdoor sports or construction work. It was a mystery, but she would get to the bottom of it. Sooner or later all things are known to a laundress.

"Hey, lady, this machine done eat my quarters. I need a refun'."

The child looked as if her clothes had been shrunk while still on her body. There was a three-inch gap between the bottom of her pink knit shirt and the top of her black knit pants. Madeleine hadn't seen her before, either with or without laundry; she smelled a scam.

"Tell me which machine it is and I'll start it for you," she replied.

"Never min'. I hear my momma callin'. I be back," blurted the girl and dashed out the door.

The laundress made the rounds between rows of machines, shutting the doors, emptying trash bins and picking up loose dryer sheets. She had to fight both the flies and several yellow jackets for possession of the Dead Mac. Then, trash stowed safely in the dumpster, she relaxed back into her niche, comforted by the thought that for perhaps another hour the place would look clean. She never hoped for more than this. Six years amidst the constant din and agitation of this place had wrung out and spun dry every ounce of ambition Madeleine had ever felt.

A slim, rolled newspaper plopped onto the counter, between two neat stacks of white t-shirts. The laundress grimaced and gingerly picked it up by one edge, to keep the ink off of the clothes and her fingers.

"Not much news in there," she stated, dropping the paper onto a stack of magazines at the end of the counter.

"You're late today, Cody. You just finishing up your route?"

"Nah. I hadda go feed my dad's cat," replied the newspaper carrier. He was not the thirteen-year-old schoolboy carrier of days gone by. He was a mid-thirties angularly framed man who wore jeans, a flannel shirt of indeterminate color, and a Boston Red Sox baseball hat turned backwards over a dark mass of curly hair. Instead of a Schwinn, he sported a vintage gray Toyota Corolla. Cody's azure eyes were bloodshot and dark circles outlined them, completing a perfectly seedy appearance.

"Your dad sure is gone a lot. Maybe you should just move in with him. Then you wouldn't have to make a special trip."

"I don't think so." Curt was Cody's modus operandi. His accent had the flavor of the northeast Atlantic seaboard, but he rarely said enough for Madeleine to pinpoint it. He nodded at a pair of men in business suits at a table in the corner and asked, "What's up with the Suits?"

"Them?" she echoed, feeling suddenly derailed from the conversation. "They're just a couple of guys on a business trip. Probably a conference or something. Why?"

"Oh, just wondering. It's not every day you see two Suits in a 'mat. Looks like they oughtta have wives in the burbs who do their stuff."

The man on the left pored over a pocket-sized spiral-bound notebook and made notes while the other man spoke to him, his right arm periodically flailing in emphasis.

"You know, now that I think about it," she mused, "they are a pretty strange pair. They sit in that corner, heads butted together like they're planning the next big bank heist. They've been in several times in the past few weeks, and each time in different clothes."

"Well, that's what you'd expect from someone in a laundromat, isn't it? You wouldn't want them to come in here buck nekkit, would-ja?" He noticed the grin broadening on her face. "Nah, never mind. Didn't anyone tell you the Seventies' free love era is over? It's 1989 already."

"No, seriously, Cody." Madeleine leaned her expansive rib cage across the counter and gripped his arm. "There *is* something odd about them. You can usually tell what folks do by the clothes they wear. These guys have a little of everything . . . suits, jeans, sports stuff, khakis, and their t-shirts have everything from Broadway shows to concrete-mixing companies on them. One of them—"

"Wait a minute," the carrier interrupted. "How do you know all this? You been inspecting their laundry bags each time they leave?"

"No, silly," she replied, aggravated. "If you'd let me finish. . .

"Sometimes they drop it off. One of them has a t-shirt that says 'FBI.' What do you think about *that*?"

"It could mean anything. I got a friend with a shirt what says CIA. Culinary Institute of America. Just because you got a shirt what says FBI don't mean you're a spook. What *you* got here is an overactive imagination. You need to get outa this job and find you something to tax your mind, like taking care of kids or something. There's tons of ads for that in the classifieds," he said, as he opened the newspaper to that section and thrust it in front of her.

"Men! You always think that child care is the answer to everything," Madeleine said, exasperated, and thrust the paper back onto the pile of magazines. She hustled another dryer load onto the counter and began to fold socks in staccato motion. "I like my job; I enjoy meeting new people and working with the public."

"You're bored stiff and the clientele ain't exactly the upper crust, doll," he said, his accent betraying a trace of New Jersey. "You're all the time watching folks and making up whole life stories about them. You think you know everything there is to know about a guy by looking at his threads or his skivvies. You don't know the first thing." He strolled over to the Coke machine, put two coins in, and made a selection. The machine rumbled, but the drink was not forthcoming.

"Damn thing," he swore and smacked it on the side. Still nothing. He walked the five paces back to the counter. Suddenly the machine came to life, and, with a series of creaks and groans, it produced a can of Coke.

"Now, if you *really* want to know what goes on in world, you oughtta be a carrier. Carriers see it all," he asserted as he popped the top on the soda.

"But you guys are only out at night, and most people are asleep at night, so how can you really say that?" Madeleine contested.

"Just because they're home don't mean they're asleep, doll. Come with me some night, and I'll show you what I mean."

"Are you serious? Me go with you on the route?" The laundress paused her folding and peered at him, unbelieving. "I'd just be in the way. And besides, what would I tell Jerry?" she asked.

"The boyfriend?" he responded. "Nah, Jerry would never even notice you're gone. Hell, he's such a wastoid, you could do a lap dance on him and he wouldn't know you were there.

"And lots of people work in twos. You'll see. Meet me at the loading dock in the back at the newspaper tonight at two. There's parking down the side of the building on the alley. And take a nap before you come. You'll need your beauty sleep."

Cody winked at her and chugged the drink down. Placing the can upright on the tile floor, he squared the ball of his foot over the can and dropped his weight down on it. The can crumpled into itself neatly until it resembled an aluminum hockey puck. He tossed it like a Frisbee into the trash and walked out.

CHAPTER 2

"Hi Jer," Madeleine said into the telephone as she wiped liquid Tide from the top of a washer. "I'm going to learn surveillance techniques tonight. Where? At the Daily Progress office in town. No, it's not exactly a class. Remember that guy who delivers the paper here? He says he can teach me how to follow people. No, they're not in here now, but they were here earlier.

"What? No, he isn't hitting on me, and no, I am not interested in him. Why do you always go there?! I just want to find out what those two guys here are up to."

She set the rag down on the machine and moved the phone to the opposite ear. She picked up the rag again and continued wiping down the row of machines.

"Unh hunh. Unh hunh. I know nobody else cares who they are or what they're doing, but *I* care. What? Of course I care about you, baby. It's only a night and I don't have to work tomorrow. We can sleep in. No, don't be ridiculous. You can live without me for one night. No, I'll be safe. I promise I won't do anything stupid."

She held the phone away from her ear and walked toward the two fifty-pound machines, both of which had just entered the final extract phase. Jerry was still clearly audible above the din.

"Gotta go, Jer—customer waiting. Bye," she said and punched the off button. Air escaped her lungs in a burst. Funny, she hadn't been aware of holding her breath.

"Hey, Rita!" Madeleine called out. A scrawny woman poked her head through rear hallway door. She wore faded jeans, an equally faded denim work shirt, and her tawny hair was tumbling out of the bun atop her head. From her hand dangled a dripping white sweater dotted with blue streaks.

7

"Yeah? What do you need? I'm working on this sweater you inked." She held out the sweater as proof. The puddle that was gathering at her feet now extended another six inches.

"I know the sweater will be spotless when you're done," said Madeleine, "but you need to make sure you don't use the mop to clean up the floor where you've dripped that bleach water."

"I know. I know. I know already! Don't mix Mr. Clean with the Clorox. I try to be helpful and this is what I get." Rita started to back through the doorway.

Madeleine rolled her eyes. "Wait! I need to ask you something," she said. "Can you work for me tomorrow morning? I'll do the drawer for you tonight. You can just close up early and go home."

"That's back-to-back shifts. What's in it for me? Overtime?" Rita asked. "I'll have to consult Eddie. You know how he feels about me doing back-to-backs."

"Oh, get real, Rita," snapped Madeleine. "Eddie doesn't give a rat's ass about anything except who's paying the cable bill. It's not a life sentence; I just want to ride along with Cody and learn what he knows about doing surveillance. He thinks those two weird guys are spies, too, and he says he can show me how to find out what they're really up to."

"Really?" Rita didn't sound very convinced. She looked at the sweater and then at the ceiling, focusing on a broken ceiling tile.

"Well, I'll do it if I can have Saturday off."

"Done!" shouted Madeleine. Then she remembered Jerry. It would be fine. Today was Tuesday. She had three days to line up a good explanation for this to Jerry.

CHAPTER 3

At 2AM nothing much was moving in downtown Charlottesville, Virginia. The bars had already rolled their patrons out, and the police had picked up those unable to walk the straight line. A few trucks trundled by, headed for the all-night grocery stores. Madeleine had never been one for the late-night scene, and this went contrary to her mental picture of it. Where were all those men in trench coats and women in hip-hugging leather miniskirts? Surely even a town of 40,000 inhabitants would have that seamy side.

She turned into the alley behind the newspaper and parked her Datsun 310 behind Cody's Toyota. On the dock Cody was deep in conversation with a slightly built, blond haired man in a yellow windbreaker. The blond man was telling a story and illustrating in silhouette hand gestures. Both men began to laugh, and several other people gravitated toward them to hear the tale. Cody called out to Madeleine to join the group, and warily she stepped up onto the dock.

"Guys, this is Mad. She's running with me tonight. It's her first time out on a route," he told them.

"Yeah, we're all a little mad around here—a little ca-razy, if you know what I mean," said the storyteller.

"And nobody knows crazy better than Potter," said an older gent, nodding at the blonde man. "They drummed him out of the city police force for being nuttier than an acorn."

"Not true, not true," Potter protested. "I was injured in the line of duty."

"Yeah, right," called a voice by the wall. "You was hit in the head and your brains done fell out."

"See what I have to put up with, lady? No respect for your boys in blue."

A bell rang and suddenly the crowd formed into a line, running from a waist-high window in the brick wall to an old Chevette parked at the end of the dock. Bulky bundles of newspapers rolled from a conveyor into Potter's waiting hands. He in turn passed them down the line until the last person chucked them into the back of the Chevette. When the last bundle for that vehicle had come down the chute, there was barely room for the three hundred-pound driver. He squeezed into his seat and backed out through a cloud of blue smoke.

The bell rang and another set of bundles rolled off the assembly. Potter inspected it and looked around.

"Who's got 225?" he asked.

"Winnie," replied a voice at the end of the line.

"Aw, hell," spouted Potter. "She's always late. Gotta clean up the church before morning prayers. Now, I ask you, just how dirty can a church get in one day?" He began stacking the bundles at the edge of the dock.

"Well, you'll never know, will you, Potter?" taunted the older man, adding, "Potter's only been to church for weddings and funerals."

"Winnie, aka 'the Church Lady,' is the preacher's wife at Free Will Christian Church," explained Cody as he passed her a bundle. "She's secretary, sexton, and self-appointed saver of souls. Basically harmless. The folks in Circulation let her fold her papers inside 'cuz nobody wants to get into a conversation with her. She might start talking about their souls. They don't let nobody else fold inside and it's beginning to irritate other carriers—if you catch my drift."

Madeleine caught it. She'd seen this principle at work many times. She often wondered if the proselytizing was simply a means to special treatment, not saving souls. Toss them a bone and maybe they'll leave you alone.

The bell pealed again and a voice called out, "260!"

"That's us," said Cody. They fed bundles into the back seat of the Corolla, until the entire rear window was blocked. Madeleine wondered whether she would fit, but there was just enough room once she took off her shoes and propped up her feet on a bundle. They pulled away from the dock and drove across town to a low-budget gas station.

While the pump was running, Cody organized his supplies. He pulled out a bag of rubber bands and speared handfuls of bands on the gearshift column. This done, he set a non-slip pad on the dash and placed a pair of scissors, a Post-It pad, and a pen on top of it. Reaching under the seat, he pulled out a pack of long plastic bags secured by a piece of cardboard with a hole in its center. He slipped a rubber band through the hole and hung the bags from the rear view mirror. The strap of bags bounced and shook as he moved about, assembling the array on the dash.

Madeleine stared at the carrier as he disappeared into the station to pay for the gas. She marveled at the disparity between his sloppy appearance and his careful placement of the items on the dash. It was a well-set table. Briefs or boxers?

CHAPTER 4

"Carriers do it in the dark. It's the first rule of newspaper carrying," said Cody as he slid into the Toyota. "You have to know where your supplies are at all times. You don't have time to be groping around for your stuff, so you always keep it in the same place. Some folks have a cup between the front seats; me, I like to keep it right where I can see it.

"The tools of the trade: a blade, a pen, Post-its, and bags. It's all here." He patted the dash as one might pat the favored dog. "Now, let's find a place to roll them up."

A few blocks down the road they pulled into the Roadside Inn parking lot and parked under a light pole. Brilliant white light flooded the interior of the car. No worries about losing anything here.

"Geez, even in the daytime, there isn't this much light in my house," Madeleine marveled.

"In my house either," said Cody. I kinda like the dark, and my dad, he's like a vampire. He's rarely up in the daytime, and when he is, he don't even stick his nose out the door.

"Pass me that bundle of papers under your feet," he said. He placed the papers on her lap and snipped the plastic band around the bundle. He replaced the scissors and began rolling up papers, securing them with rubber bands, and laying them in the space between himself and Madeleine. She followed suit and soon the stack was up to their elbows.

"Is this enough to start us?" Madeleine asked as she rolled the last paper in her lap.

"Hell, no!" he snorted. "Pull up that other bundle on the floor." She did and he repeated the process, only

this time he pulled a sheet of computer printout paper off
the top of the bundle. He read through it and used the pen
from the dash to jot a few notes on the printout. Madeleine
was surprised to see that, even though the array was set up
in the center of the dash, Cody wrote the notes left-handed.
He was a "Southpaw."

"The freebies are payin' off on Pear St. I been
tossing them in that new Orchard Village subdivision, and
Circulation got three new customers on that street. Won't
be long before I have the whole sub locked up. That's
eighty, if I'm lucky. I ain't seen the competition in there
yet," he said while he penned notes to his new customers
on the Post-it pad.

Attaching each yellow note to a rolled paper, Cody
set them on the dash. Then he pulled the strap of plastic
bags down and tugged at the top bag, so that it opened
slightly. He picked up a newspaper roll from the dash and
slid it down into the plastic bag so neatly that it looked
vacuum-sealed. He encircled the suspended bag with his
fingers and pushed upward forcing out any remaining air,
then twirled and yanked the bag from the strap. In a flash
he had tied it off and slapped it back on the dash.

"Okay, doll," he said, "let's roll a few more and you
can fill me in on the Suits while we roll."

"The Suits are staying at the Doubletree, rooms 203
and 205," reported Madeleine. "And they've been there for
at least three weeks. One day they'll come in dressed in T-
shirts and jeans all covered in dust or paint. The next day
they show up in pin-stripe suits, looking like something off
of Wall Street. And when they do it themselves, they always
sit in the corner and talk all hush-hush. You saw them.
They sit with their heads together like lovers and, talk about
the hand gestures, the older one could do interpretation for
the deaf."

"Man, that's gotta cost them a pretty penny," said

the carrier. "I understand doing drop-off, but I just don't get why they do it themselves. It don't make sense. If they can afford to stay at the Doubletree, why the hell do self-serve? Maybe it's time you got nosey—put some of that God-given talent to work. Meantime, we can go check out the hotel an' see if they got any late-night habits. I got a customer next door, so we can park in his lot an' bag the next batch while we window-shop.

"Here, put these papers on the floor an' grab another batch outa the back seat." With that, he turned on the engine, jerked the car into reverse, and raced out of the parking lot, alternately thrusting Madeleine between the seats and back against the dash. Her bosom felt compressed from a 36D to a 34B. Add this experience to the list of preparations for a person's first mammogram, she thought.

When she finally got her bearings again and had the new bundle safely in her lap, she noticed that the place setting on the dash was exactly as it had been when they left the gas station. Either that rubber pad worked very well or Cody was really quick on the draw.

CHAPTER 5

"Oh, my God! Did you see that?" exclaimed Madeleine, jabbing her finger against the windshield. "That guy's driving the wrong way down the street and he's running along the curb!" The green Ford Escort wagon was indeed moving in a jerky fashion down the left side of the street. Cody was unperturbed.

"That's Bob. He's one of us. He's filling tubes. Usually he's got Ellen along and she can get the tubes from the other side. But if it's only one person delivering, you gotta take a few liberties to get the job done. We run on both sides of the street when we need to. Sometimes other folks think we're toasted and do their civic duty and call the cops. By law the cops gotta check it out. But they know us, and mostly it's a formality. Some carriers think it helps to put a Day-Glo orange magnetic sign on the back of their vehicles. 'Caution: Frequent Stops: Newspaper Delivery'. I don't usually, except when I get a new set 'o wheels."

"How often is that?" asked Madeleine. She rolled and banded papers while he talked. It was like folding laundry: an easy, familiar rhythm. The pile of newspapers gradually filled up the space around her legs.

"Most carriers get new wheels every other year. But me, I don't drive nothin' but Toyota, so I'm usually good for three. Now, Betty, she's exceptional. We been partners for four years," Cody patted the dash affectionately. "Four years, about a hundred miles a night, seven days a week—and we haven't missed once."

17

"Jeez, don't you guys ever get a day off or a vacation?"

"Some folks call in sick and some folks have a friend or relative what takes the route so they can go off for a couple days. I'm the relief carrier when there's a no-show."

Madeleine sighed. She knew all about being the "relief pitcher." Managing a laundromat meant doing a lot of extra shifts. Some people called in sick; others called in drunk. Some never called at all. Right now it was just herself and Rita, a bad situation if Rita got sick.

"How do you manage to fit in more than one route in a night?" she asked. "A hundred miles would take all night to do."

"Lots of the routes cross each other," he replied. "I might go up one side of a street and another carrier go down the other; or I might go half way down both sides of a street and another carrier pick up where I stop, and go to the end of the road. It seems crazy, but it works out when you have to dump an extra route on another carrier.

"Each of us makes a tape of our route and the office keeps a copy in case something happens. The substitute plugs the tape into the tape player and gets a little commentary all the way along the route. Some carriers list tubes and tosses, road names and route numbers; others gotta tell you every little niggly detail. And we got a few what wanna be comedians."

"I get it—instead of doing 'stand-up', they're doing sit-down," quipped the laundress.

"Har, har, har," he said dryly. "Looks like you're burying yourself in your work there."

Madeleine paused, rubber band poised to slide down a rolled paper. The papers were stacked up to her waist and stuffed into the well between herself and the door. On Cody's side the papers were spilling higglty-pigglty around the gearshift.

18

"Tsk tsk," he chided softly, and straightened up the mess, one paper at a time. Briefs or boxers?

CHAPTER 6

Turning onto a nearly deserted fast food alley, he barreled toward the interstate. Doubletree Hotel loomed in front of them, six floors of beige concrete without a hint of arboreal relief. He circled the structure and then pulled into the IHOP next door.

"This won't take long. How about you roll about thirty while I transact a little business. And you better put your shoes on now while you can still find them," Cody instructed.

Taking a bundle from the back of the vehicle, the carrier approached the line of metal stands by the door. He opened the far-right newspaper box, removed a paper, and replaced it with the bundle. His long fingers dove into a left pants pocket, producing a penknife with which he cut the strap. He pulled out the strap and let the lid spring shut. Cody disappeared into the IHOP, dropping the strap into the waste can as he passed. Through the glass panes Madeleine could see him talking to a man at the cash register. The man shook his head in response and then reached under the counter and passed a small bundle to Cody.

Moments later Cody returned with a smile upon his face. He chucked the bundle he'd received from the man into the trunk area and resumed his seat, making a short note on his printout. Madeleine was tiring of the bagging experience. Itching to move on to actual delivery, she descended on him with a torrent of questions.

"That took a while. Who was that man? What were you talking about? What did he hand you? I thought we were going to stake those two guys out. How are we going to have time to do that? We haven't even started to deliver the papers!"

"Whoa, Nelly!" he countered, "Now that's watcha call shrill. Girl, you could send the junkyard dog running with that voice.

"The answers are: Fayed owns this IHOP. I was quizzing him about the Suits. What he handed me was yesterday's returns—that's unsold papers, to you. And, we got a bunch more papers to roll before we roll. Delivery is the quick part. It's all in the prep. I usually ride alone, but with you riding shotgun, it'll go real fast once we get the prep done. Any more questions?"

Madeleine stared at her red rubber sneaker toes. She wondered if her face matched the rubber. Was it possible to teleport back to the laundromat? She smacked her toes together three times and mentally repeated "no place like home," but to no avail.

"What did Fayed say?" she asked in her smallest voice.

"Relax. I don't wanna spend time speculatin' when somebody else might be able to tell me what I wanna know. And Fayed is a gold mine of information. He sees everybody and he gots a nose for trouble. Because this IHOP is right behind the Doubletree, it gets a lot of their business. Just made sense to check him out first."

Cody bagged three papers and removed the empty strap from the mirror. He dropped the old cardboard on the floor and pulled a fresh strap from under the seat. He ignored Madeleine's rapidly tapping foot and calmly positioned the new strap.

"Now, what he said is *very* interesting. Fayed thinks they're gay, but he thinks that about any two guys who come in late and act that chummy. He wondered the same thing you did, 'bout their profession. He's gonna keep an eye out for me. Now, let's go roll the rest o' these babies."

CHAPTER 7

Cody pulled Betty around to the rear of the restaurant and parked next to a silver Lexus. He opened up the back door, reorganized the papers so that Madeleine again had bundles under her feet and the rolled papers were now stacked on the floor behind them.

"I know you want things to move faster, like the 007 flicks," Cody said, "but it don't work that way in real life. If you got patience, sooner or later they'll tip their hand. An' catching them means just bein' there to see it happen. Everything has to look like normal. If all of a sudden we vary the routine, somebody'll notice, and somebody'll say somethin', and somebody'll hear them say it. You catch my drift?

"You think something's funky with these guys. So do I, but so far we don't got squat to go on, but their threads and using a 'mat to meet in. Maybe if we watch, we'll see something. Meantime, we got two hundred papers to roll, so pull out another bundle."

Madeleine was relieved to go back to rolling papers. It gave her something to focus on besides her humiliation and the knot in her stomach.

"You obviously never asked them what line of work they're in. How come?" asked the carrier.

"They weren't exactly chatty. I could never get a good lead in," said Madeleine, recalling the day they first entered her establishment. "They were all business. They wanted to know turn-around time. Could I get it done today? Could they pick it up this afternoon? No, tonight will definitely be too late. They wanted special treatment. Could I get this stain out? Red wine off a white shirt? Sure, but maybe not by this afternoon. Well, exactly how hard *is* it to get the stain out? What takes so long?

"They didn't seem to notice that I was practically swimming in drop-off. I explained to them that I do a hundred pounds a shift by myself, keep the place clean, and wait hand-and-foot on people like them." She paused. Cody's head was turned toward the window, and his shoulders were heaving.

"You are laughing at me, you bum!" She slapped at him with a banded paper.

"Mad, if you could see that Queen Shaniqua look on your face. You even got that head-swivel thing going." he said and threw up his arms in self-defense.

Through the windshield they had a clear view of the hotel rooms as they rolled newspapers. Madeleine pointed out their car, a navy blue Crown Victoria, parked near the corner by the office. She counted the rooms and identified rooms 203 and 205. Room 203 was dark but room 205 was lit. The curtains were open a crack and a man was seated at a table, working on a laptop computer. Blue light glowed from his screen as he typed.

"I wish I could see what he's writing," sighed the laundress. I can't even tell which one of them it is."

"You mean you didn't bring your opera glasses?" Cody laughed and produced a pair of binoculars from under the seat. He hung them in the air in front of Madeleine's nose and she snatched them from his hand eagerly.

"Wow! It's the younger one, the straight haired guy with the big mouth. I still can't see what he's typing. Shoot! He just closed it up. Now we'll never know." She put the field glasses down in her lap and watched the man draw the curtain shut. "Do you think he knows we're watching him?"

"Nah," replied the carrier. "It's three-thirty in the morning. He's going beddie-bye. Even spooks gotta get some shut-eye. And no, that don't mean I think they *are* spooks. They're still just a couple of suits on a business trip, far as I can see."

"So much for your surveillance methods," said Madeleine, handing back the glasses. She picked up a paper and rolled it listlessly.

"Aw, come on," Cody said and winked at her. "Rome weren't built in a day. Maybe we'll get lucky tomorrow night. Think you can get another night off from your ole man?"

"Not without him thinking I'm having an affair. He thinks I'm sleeping around every time I go to the movies with a girlfriend. I don't like to hear him whine, so I don't go out much anymore."

Cody studied her for a minute and then asked, "You two ever go out together? He ever take you dancing or out to eat?"

She shook her head. "We used to go out a lot. Then Jerry got laid off his job and it took all my paycheck to cover the bills. I don't mind that much. I can read or watch the tube. It's easier that way."

"Death by TV. It wouldn't work for me, but if that's what floats your boat, so be it." He put the binoculars back under the seat and started the engine. "Let's blow this Popsicle stand."

For the next two hours they drove up one street and down another, stuffing newspaper tubes and tossing bagged papers onto driveways. With each neighborhood Cody went through a short litany of special and persnickety customers. Mrs. Moss had to have her paper right at the door because she was elderly and afraid of falling down the three steps to her front walk. Mr. Shifflett had a pair of Rottweilers who patrolled his yard and might take your arm off if you missed the toss over the high fence. Better not to miss.

Some of the neighborhoods were mostly apartment complexes and Madeleine discovered that her summers as a softball player paid off handsomely. With a little practice she could accurately lob a paper up a flight of stairs to her target. What was hard was mastering the delicate balance of an accurate but soundless toss. Cody was so well-practiced in this art that his tosses produced only a slight "plop."

About five-thirty they rounded the corner by Madeleine's laundromat. At Madeleine's request they stopped for a quick break. The silence inside was broken only by a constant drip of a leaky faucet from the back hall.

"This is the first time I ever been here that there wasn't thirty machines going and a gang of kids in an out the door," Cody observed. "It's kinda nice."

"Yeah," answered Madeleine as she flicked through the previous day's receipts. "I am going to have to talk to that girl."

"What girl?"

"Rita," she responded, as if that explained everything. She tapped her fingers on the counter absently. "I think she's borrowing from the drawer again.

"She always has a flawless drawer—until the end of the month. Then she's short three times in a week. Dang if it doesn't add up to fifty bucks every time.

"I guess I shouldn't be mad. It used to be a lot worse. She used to put stuff up her nose and that was very expensive. Whole deposits disappeared until I relieved her of the responsibility of taking the deposit to the bank. It took her two years to pay it back." Madeleine ran a hand through her hair and then put the receipts in a box on the counter.

"Most folks woulda canned her butt. How come you didn't?" asked Cody. He fished in his jeans for some change. "Wanna Coke?"

"No, thanks," answered the laundress and sighed, "What I want is coffee and a new life.

"Managing employees is the biggest pain in the ass." Madeleine settled into the barstool behind the counter. "Rita is really a great attendant in a lot of ways. She always shows up for her shift. She isn't fazed by big loads or really grimy drop-off. In fact, she has a macho thing about how much drop-off she can do per shift. It's rare to find someone like that. But she hates to clean and she has this obnoxious borrowing habit.

"I'll bet you that Coke or a cup of java that she hasn't hosed out the soap bins all week, and that she's left a mop bucket full of Mr. Clean and filthy water—with an open bottle of bleach on the shelf next to it." She folded her arms across her chest and smiled smugly.

"So what if she leaves the mop bucket out? I don't get it," said Cody. He put two quarters in and smacked the side of the machine. The drink rolled out and he popped the tab. Then he peered into the back and sure enough, it was exactly as Madeleine had described.

"Did she lock the back door?" asked Madeleine.

A rumbling sound issued from the rear, followed by a loud bang. Cody was laughing as he returned. "She ever blame the disappearing till on burglars?"

"Once, and that was when I threatened to call the police and get the drawer checked for fingerprints. We'd all been sick, so I gloved up and cleaned the whole place top to bottom. I knew the only prints on it would be hers. But she still leaves that door unlocked sometimes. It's a pain. You have to push it shut from the outside and then come back in and jerk on it until the bolt can go into the slide. Sometimes I have to take a hammer and bang on the bolt to make it move. If it was any easier to get it open or shut we'd have been burgled a long time ago. And that's her saving grace."

Cody took a long draw on his soda. "I give, but I still don't get the part about the bucket."

Madeleine stared at him unbelieving. "You're kidding. Don't you know that when you mix bleach and ammonia you make chlorine gas?"

"It don't say nothing on the label about chlorine gas," he responded.

"I know. It tells you not to mix strong chemicals, but it doesn't say which ones or why. You're supposed to know that already. Didn't your mother ever teach you that?"

"Let's leave my mother out of it," he said. "How bad is chlorine gas?"

"If you're standing there when the bottle of bleach falls into the bucket of mop water, you can kiss your ass goodbye. Any amount can start the reaction, and in a closed space it's deadly. I can't tell you how many times I've blasted Rita for that, and still she doesn't pay attention. I expect some morning I'll find her dead on the floor back here.

"So now that we've had our chemistry lesson for the day, let's go get that java you owe me," Madeleine said with a wink.

CHAPTER 8

But java was not next. As they pulled out of the parking lot, three police cars flew by, lights flashing. The first flipped its siren on as a warning to the Corolla, and then continued silently on its way.

"I wonder what the fuss is all about," mused Cody. "The rest of my route is in that direction. Let's mosey on behind them and check it out. We can get coffee later. It's probably a domestic or a B&E—but maybe not."

He followed the lights and soon rounded a corner onto the street where Madeleine had spotted the green Escort wending its way along the curb. A police cruiser closed off the intersection at the end of the block and two officers manned the checkpoint. Though most of the houses had a few lights on and either faces peering from the windows or someone out on the front porch, the third house from the end, a modest brick Victorian was lit up from top to bottom. Through the oval shaped window on its front porch Madeleine saw an elderly woman in curlers and pink housecoat weeping and gesturing as two policemen took her statement.

Cody came slowly up to the blockade and rolled down his window.

"Got business in this neighborhood, Cody?" asked the officer.

"Nope. Just passing through. Rest of my route is out in the county. What's going on?"

The officer shined a long black mag light in Madeleine's face. She winced. He angled the beam to catch every surface in the vehicle and then snapped it off.

"You got a new partner?"

"Maybe. She's scouting a new profession. Jury's still out."

"Well, tonight's not a good night to be scouting. We've just had two B&E's in this neighborhood, and another three blocks away. I expect your newsroom to be descending on us any minute. That toad in the Escort is always the first to blab the good news."

"Bob?" asked Cody, more to himself than to the officer. "Was it one of his customers?"

"Turns out no, but he had to stop to ask. Saw the lights, knew the neighborhood. I hate that guy. If he didn't have a legit reason for being here, he'd be the first on my list of suspects.

"You two go on and run your route. If anything turns up, you can read about it in tomorrow's paper, just like everybody else."

"See ya, dude," replied Cody, taking no offense. He rolled up the window and headed down the street.

"How're you holding up?" he asked the laundress.

"Depends on how long it is until I get that cup of java. The adrenaline is only good for so long. How long does it take to do the rest?" she asked.

"An hour or so. Let's just zip on it and I'll getcha a mondo mocha." He gave her no chance to reply. He stepped on the gas and Betty sped off into the sunrise.

CHAPTER 9

"So how did you're class go last night," asked Rita. "Are those guys spies?"

"Maybe. We don't know yet," said Madeleine. "Cody's got a friend watching them too, and he's as suspicious about them as we are." She counted the tens in the till again.

"You have any trouble with the drawer today?" she asked Rita.

"No." Rita's arms went rigid at her sides, her head tipped backward slightly, and her eyes narrowed. "It was exactly on the money when I counted out."

"And that was an hour ago. It's off $10 now," said Madeleine. "Did you make change or sell any quarter rolls?"

Rita's hands clenched into fists and then slowly unclenched. Her lips smiled but the eyes remained slits. "No," she replied flatly.

"It's the second time this week. I know you have insurance to pay on Fridays, but this isn't the way to do it," said Madeleine. "From now on, first shift counts the drawer when second shift gets here. Then second shift counts it. Get it? Got it? Good."

"I've worked for you for how many years and you think I would steal from you?" Rita was gearing up to her Jewish-mother routine. "So that's the thanks I get for switching shifts with you. If it was just me, I could take the heat. It wouldn't matter, but I have Eddie to think of. He— "

"Can it, Rita," Madeleine cut her off. "Remember those deposits that you borrowed? Yes, I see you do. You're lucky I didn't prosecute you for that. I think the legal term is embezzlement. I've been keeping track of your borrowing since then, and it's getting to be a hefty sum.

31

Let's see . . . at fifty bucks a month for the last six months, that's three hundred dollars."

The laundress thought fast. Surely Rita wouldn't want to drag out her punishment. And with Rita covering first shift, Madeleine could work second and also do surveillance with Cody on his route. Jerry was still an issue, but she would deal with him later.

"Would you prefer me to take it out of your paycheck or would you rather take a few shifts for me. I'd say you owe me five shifts at this point. Which is it going to be?"

"All right," Rita said, eyes wary but defiance beginning to melt from her arms. "I'll cover your shifts, but it doesn't mean I'm admitting anything about embezzling. And I don't know what I'm going to tell Eddie."

"You can quit playing your guilt card," said Madeleine. "I don't care if you tell Eddie you're doing the shifts because I'm working with the police to uncover a ring of burglars." Her voice rose triumphant.

Across the room a chair scraped the floor. The rotund woman in sweatshirt and skin-tight knit pants previously seated there was now hurling her clothes, still wet, from a dryer into her basket.

"Or," Madeleine lowered her voice to a stage whisper, "you can tell him we're on the trail of international spies!"

CHAPTER 10

Jerry was pacing, and none too steady on his feet. The Old Milwaukee in his hand tilted at a dangerous angle as he used it to punctuate his slurred words.

"Iss cold in this house, an' you didn't come home las' night," he said.

"I did come home this morning, and I slept in that bed with you. You were still out like a light when I went to work this afternoon," Madeleine replied, adding, "You could have turned the heat on."

"Iss not the same. I need you with me. How do I know you're not out there makin' love wi' the news . . . paper guy. Wha's his name?"

He tripped on the edge of the rug and fell against Madeleine. She reached out and grabbed the brown glass bottle as it left his fingers. Setting the bottle on a side table next to her, she circled her arm around his waist. Together they weaved toward the couch and sat. Madeleine disentangled her arm and looked at her man. He was already snoring.

She picked up the remote and turned on the TV. "Columbo" was airing on A&E Network. Pulling the afghan over her, she settled in to watch Peter Falk quizzing Ruth Gordon. Though it was her favorite show and her favorite episode, she couldn't seem to lose herself in it tonight. Red rubber toes tapped as her thoughts flitted between the various dramas of her life.

Was Jerry ever going to cut back his drinking and get another job? Would she ever see the man she used to know and love? Did she still love him? Images of a future of cleaning up beer spittle from a wizened old man flashed in front of her. It was too depressing. So was the thought of him driving while sipping yet another six-pack of Old

Milwaukee. She steered her mind away from that line of thought.

And what about that business with Rita? God, that woman was a piece of work! Rita acted like you were best friends and all the while she was robbing you blind. She deserved that old couch potato husband of hers.

Madeleine looked again at Jerry, who was slumping deeper and deeper into the opposite corner of the sofa. Maybe she shouldn't be so judgmental about who deserved whom. What had *she* done to deserve this?

Memories arose of twelve-step meetings where well-meaning people tried to convince her that she was not the source of the problem. She was beginning to believe them. Surely nothing she had tried had worked, not the reasoning with him, the pleading, or the dumping his beer down the sink. Every time things got really bad and she threatened to throw him out, he would suddenly turn over a new leaf. The old Jerry would return and she'd get her hopes up again. It was an old story, one told countless times over countless cups of coffee after the meetings.

One could never count on things happening as planned, so after a while there was no incentive to plan anything, do anything, go anywhere. Whatever the tales were, they all agreed on one thing: the lies were the worst. Take the time Jerry came home, after three days of sobriety, with every pore reeking of alcohol, and yet he claimed that he'd only had a single beer. Who was the bigger fool, him for thinking she believed him, or her for believing he would change some day?

Again Madeleine's mind balked and sent her spinning in another direction. The Suits. The Men In Black. What was that man typing in his lap-top last night? What was their mission? She wondered if he'd be typing again tonight. What was she doing, sitting here when she could be tracking down spies?

"Excuse me. You wouldn't happen to recall . . . ?"

Peter Falk was asking his trademark question. Madeleine punched the remote and he disappeared into black screen. She heaved her bulk off the couch, lifted the snoring man's feet into her spot and covered him with the afghan. Maybe she should get some sleep before she headed downtown. As her head hit the pillow upstairs, she thought if she could only get a look at that computer. . . she could be in and out before Jerry ever woke up. He would never have to know. Now was not the time to rock the boat.

CHAPTER 11

The group at the dock was smaller than on the previous night. The old geezer was leaning against the brick wall, tucking a pinch of snuff into his lower lip. Several carriers stood staring through a large plate glass window above them. Images and lines of printed matter blurred together as the rolls of paper raced through the presses behind the glass. Cody was nowhere in sight.

"She's back!" shouted Potter over his shoulder when Madeleine mounted the platform. He turned back to her. "So, do you like the newspaper business . . . or is it my stunning good looks?"

"Better watch out, Mad," advised the elderly carrier from the opposite end of the dock. "Pretty soon they'll be placing bets on whether or not you're a long- or short-timer. The average lifetime for a carrier in this place is about three months. Me, I always bet on the underdog."

"Don't let these guys fill your head with a lotta crap, doll," said a familiar voice behind her. Cody nodded toward his car at the far end of the alley. "Let's get ready."

She opened the passenger side door and cleared a space to sit. Cody busied himself with the strap of bags and his placemat.

"Jerry know you're here?" he asked.

"No," she said.

"You gonna tell him?"

"Not unless he asks," she answered. Her face was getting hot. Maybe this wasn't such a good idea after all.

"Yeah, never volunteer anything. It's a good policy.

"So, anything new on the Suits?"

"Nope. Haven't seen hide nor hair of them. Maybe tonight we'll get to see what they're up to on that laptop."

"Patience, Grasshoppa," said Cody as he placed his pen on the dash. "You don't ketch no fish by chasing them with a net. You put the net in the water and wait. And we got plenty of time to wait."

"But they could leave town tomorrow, and then we'd never know what they're up to," countered Madeleine.

"They got any laundry to pick up? Any dry cleaning?"

A smile spread across the laundress's face as she remembered a navy three-piece suit and pale yellow silk tie, due back on Friday. The younger Suit would be back for that tie.

"Yep. The young one has a thing for silk. We have until Friday anyway. That's when his suit and tie are due in."

"Good," said Cody. The o's cascaded from his lips, creating two syllables in a deep guttural tone.

Madeleine looked up. This was the sound of an animal on the prowl. He wanted to catch these spies. *He* wanted it as much as she did. This was no academic exercise. It was a hunt. And it was good.

Cody finished his prep work and put Betty into gear. He gassed up at the Lucky Seven and got two coffees during his stop at the IHOP. From their stake-out position behind the restaurant, they watched lights go on and off in the hotel windows. The curtains were open in Room 205 but the lights were off.

"Do you still have those binoculars handy, Cody?" asked Madeleine. He pulled them out from under his seat and passed them to her.

"Don't think you're gonna see much. Looks like nobody's home, and if they're up to somethin,' they're not likely to leave it out for the maid to see."

The laundress set the binoculars on the dash and surveyed the bundles and piles of wrapped newspapers. There were still at least a hundred left to do.

"Well, they have to come back sometime, so we might as well work here as anywhere else."

"You know, Fayed could be right. Maybe they're shacked up in 203 together," suggested Cody.

"I don't think so," said Madeleine. "I've got pretty good gaydar and they don't seem the type. They might huddle in the corner at the laundromat, but it looks more like business than pleasure. They're hatching something and it isn't a love affair."

She picked up a bundle and began rolling papers again. Cody gave her a stack of inserts for a special bundle.

"What are these for?" she asked, not bothering to read them.

"They're for the Orchard Village sub. I give them ten freebies and this is the invitation to subscribe. After that, they gotta pay. Usually ten days is all it takes to get 'em hooked."

"Geez, you sound like a drug dealer. Are you sure this is all you sell?"

"I been known to smoke some weed, but sellin' takes too much time an' it's too much risk. I don't want nobody knocking on my door, leastwise the cops. You hear what they call guys like that? 'Toads.' I ain't nobody's toad."

Madeleine was about to ask Cody why this was such a big deal when a familiar navy blue Crown Victoria pulled into the lot opposite them and parked. She tapped his thigh and whispered "Sh-h-h!" Together they stared as the two Suits disembarked and entered the hotel. Madeleine grabbed the binoculars and trained them on Room 205. Moments later blue light filled the window and the occupant was seated at his laptop.

"Can you read anything?" Cody asked.

"No, I can't make anything out. Maybe it's the angle of the screen. Here, you try." She handed him the glasses.

"Hmm . . . somethin', somethin' . . . colonel's underwear . . . matter of national security . . ." He threw up his arm to ward off the repeated blows from a tightly wrapped newspaper. "I'm serious! I ain't makin' it up. Here. Lean over this way and see for yourself."

Madeleine hiked herself up against the brake lever and took the binoculars. After twisting her body several directions proved unsuccessful, she scooted across the lever and against Cody's lean frame, pushed aside the strap of bags dangling from the mirror and looked again. Cody let the brake down gently and held her arms to steady her. She rotated the adjustment dial over her nose and the blue screen came into focus. Madeleine's heart began to pound and it sang in her ears. She saw the same words Cody had seen, but they made no sense. She strained to see more but the typist was blocking the view. A few seconds later the screen went blank and the man drew the curtains shut.

The scent of Irish Spring soap filled her nostrils. Madeleine became aware of the hands that were still holding her steady and the heat that was building in the scant space between their bodies. She wanted to sink down into his arms like a warm bubble bath. This is madness, she thought. She felt ashamed. It was what Jerry had always expected of her. She slid her bulk back into the passenger seat and hauled up a new bundle to roll.

Cody studied the laundress, whose attention was now riveted on the stack of newspapers in her lap. Her red rubber-toed sneakers were tapping rapidly under a growing pile of paper tubes. A smile grew at the corners of his mouth. She had forgotten to add the inserts and he bet it didn't have a thing to do with the Suits. He picked up the inserts, wrapped one around each of the papers Madeleine had just banded, and dropped them into the bags hanging from the mirror.

"So who is the Colonel and whadda you think it meant, the 'matter of national security'?" Cody asked. He twirled a bag and tied it off.

"I have no idea," said Madeleine, thinking that somehow everything in her life these days boiled down to boxers or briefs . . . or commando.

"Maybe he's smuggling secret documents in his underwear," she ventured, happy to be back on solid ground with her spy theory.

"Nah," said Cody. "It's too obvious. Nobody does that."

"And how would *you* know that, Mr. Smarty-pants Newspaper Carrier?" she replied. "And besides, if you think that nobody would ever believe you'd do the obvious, then they're not going to look there."

"You might have a point there." The carrier counted the papers with the extra sheet and stacked them in the well between himself and Madeleine.

"Okay, let's book."

The Orchard subdivision was dark and quiet. Betty rolled

up one street and down another until Cody spied a bagged newspaper at the foot of a driveway.

"Took 'em long enough," he mumbled to himself and pulled the brake up. He opened the door, retrieved the bag and stared at it.

"Son of a bitch! It's one of ours. It's that weasel Bob's. How'd he get into *my* territory?"

Cody rolled down his window and put Betty into gear. He stacked his lap with bagged papers and began tossing them as he moved clockwise through the subdivision. Madeleine watched in silence as the papers fell with a slap, not a plop. She had never seen this side of her friend. In ten minutes he covered all eighty driveways and retrieved each of the other carrier's papers. He steered Betty back onto the highway and headed for town.

"Boss Man and me are gonna have a little talk," he said. Madeleine wasn't sure if he was directing the remark toward herself or to Betty, so she said nothing. The only sound in the old Toyota was a rhythmic rustle of paper tubes on the floor.

CHAPTER 12

"I got some vanishing cream for those dark circles you're growin'," said Rita. "You sure you want to keep doing second shift?"

"Not until you've worked off that three hundred dollars," replied Madeleine. She checked her reflection in the dryer door glass. Rita was right about the shadows around her eyes, but Madeleine was not about to agree with her. Anyway, it was only for a few more days.

"And what does Jerry have to say about you traipsing around at all hours of the night with Cody?" Rita's head was beginning the Queen Shaniqua swivel.

"You can forget the blackmail angle. I already told Jerry what we're doing. And besides, it's none of your frickin' business what I tell Jerry. Since when did you care about his feelings? When you wanted time off from Eddie and we went to the movies, Jerry thought we were doing the lesbian thing. Remember? Remember what you said about Jerry's feelings then?"

Madeleine examined the drop-off bag on the counter and slid a stack of folded socks down bedside the t-shirts. She picked the bag up and bounced it several times on the counter, pressed the top down and tied it off. It was a perfect cube of clean laundry. She looked across the counter at Rita. Rita was busy searching her hair for split ends.

"You wanted to make out at the front door to see if Jerry could actually get up off the couch. How nice was *that*? Wasn't it you who said 'Fuck him if he can't take a joke'?"

"All right already! I get it! So, what happened last night? Did you find anything out about those guys?"

"Yeah," said Madeleine, "but I don't know what it means. They're up to something and it's definitely big."

At the end of the line of mid-sized washers the extract cycle ended, shifting the noise level from ear-splitting bearing whine to TV talk show mumble. She lowered her voice. "There's a Colonel involved and it's a matter of national security." No need to tell Rita that it was also a matter of the Colonel's underwear.

Madeleine filled out the drop-off ticket and made an entry into the log. She grabbed a couple trash bags and walked across the room to empty the forty-five gallon trash can.

"Did you hear anything about the burglaries the other night?" she asked Rita.

"What burglaries?" Rita said through the strings of tawny hair she was trimming. Wisps of hair drifted to her feet.

"Oh, yeah, I forgot. I took the paper home with me, so maybe you didn't get to read it," said Madeleine. She set the trash bag outside the door and started on the other can.

"There were some houses burgled on Alderman Road. The police had the road blocked off and were asking Cody all kinds of questions. I'm going to keep my eyes open when we're out tonight. Maybe I'll see something. There's all kinds of stuff you can see while you're running a route. Cody's right. We could be the next Peale and Steed."

Rita's eyes glazed over. She yawned and replaced the scissors in the drawer. "Who are Pead and Steele?" she asked.

"John Steed and Emma Peale. You know, with the canes? 'The Avengers' on PBS." She brandished an imaginary cane. "I thought you watched TV. I guess you just watch soaps. Anyway, they solve mysteries and break spy rings," stated Madeleine, careful to omit that her favorite aspect of the show was the sophisticated sexual undercurrent between the two characters.

"Can I clock out?" asked Rita.

"Yeah, but sweep up that hair before you go. I'm

44

not paying you to cut your hair here." The laundress finished bagging the trash and loaded the bags into the dumpster outside.

As Madeleine opened the front door, a customer backed through the opening with a heavily laden basket of wet clothes. Madeleine held the door and asked, as the rotund woman from the previous day passed by her, "Did you get a dryer at home?"

The customer's Dr. Scholl's clogs clop-clop-clopped as she traversed the parking lot. She did not acknowledge Madeleine. Instead, she squeezed between Madeleine's car and a green Ford Escort, up-ending the basket so she could shove it into the back seat of the Escort. Then she heaved her own bulk into the driver's seat and sped out of the lot.

Leaning against the front window, the laundress folded her arms across her bosom and watched the Escort disappear. There was something about that car. She turned back toward the counter. There must be a million cars like that.

"F-O-R-D." She sounded out the initials. "Fix Or Repair Daily."

"More like 'Found On the Road Dead,'" said a voice from the back. Cody strode through the rear hallway door and dropped a newspaper on the counter. "Forget something?"

"How long have you been here? Were you listening in on us? How the hell did you get in?" Hands on hips, jaw thrust out, red-rubber toe tapping, she was about to lay into him but stopped short.

"Damn that girl! Rita left the door open again, didn't she!" the laundress fumed.

"You really oughtta put an alarm on that thing. You know what she does out there? She steps out there to catch a little buzz. Now I can see by the look on your face you think she's just having a smoke, but didn't you ever notice the smell on her? And sometimes she transacts business back there."

"What business?'

"Don't be dense, Mad. She ain't selling drop-off," Cody's voice dropped an octave. "She's selling weed."

"In *my* laundromat? Why that rotten little twerp!"

"Chill out, doll," Cody interrupted. "You need that twerp to cover your butt so we can run surveillance."

"What if I get busted because she's running drugs through my business?" Madeleine ran a hand through her mane. Getting high on the job was one thing; selling the stuff was a whole other matter.

"The feds ain't interested in you," answered the carrier.

"How would *you* know? And how do you know she's dealing?"

"I got my sources, and no, I didn't buy nothin' off her.

"Hey, Mad, I need a favor. Can you put up my dad's cat for a couple days? I gotta do some stuff and I don't want him in my way."

"Sure," she replied, "but why not just shut the cat in a bedroom?"

"It's complicated, what I'm doing, and I gotta be in and outa the rooms. So it really don't work to put him in one. You think Jerry'll mind?"

"Jerry will never even notice he's there. These days he doesn't notice much except his beer."

"I'll bet he notices when *you're* not there," Cody commented. He unwrapped the paper and scanned the headlines. Then he flipped to the back page of Section A and scanned it. "That's good," he said to himself.

"What's good?" asked the laundress.

"None of the people what got burgled are our customers."

"You mean none of them are *your* customers," she corrected.

"Nah, *our* customers," he replied. "I know everybody's route, and they ain't ours." Cody folded up the paper and set it on the counter.

"Guess I better head out. I gotta hit Radio Shack and Food Lion. How's about I pick you up tonight and drop off Cosmo at the same time?

"Later, doll," he said and winked.

Cody turned his baseball cap backwards and strode through the front door without waiting for a response. Madeleine went into the back room and checked the heavy steel door. The door was locked and bolted. Outside she could hear Betty coming to life. He must have parked on the side street, she thought. She wondered if the back door had been wide open when he arrived or if he had just tried it to see if it was open and got lucky. And how the hell did he get it shut without her hearing the bang? Best not to think about it too much. Thinking about Cody was beginning to bring on those sensations that get one into trouble. And trouble was not what she needed right now.

She capped the Clorox and set it in its cubby. She made another mental hatch mark on her list of grievances. When this was all over, she was going to have a long talk with Rita.

CHAPTER 13

Cody's knock was just a soft rasp at one-thirty. He bore a beige plastic carrier in one hand and a maroon litter box in the other.

"You got a couple soup bowls?" he asked.

"Sounds like he's moving in," replied Madeleine. "You're not planning to dump him on me, are you? Jerry doesn't like cats."

"Nah. This project won't take long—fifteen, maybe twenty minutes. I just gotta be able to move around unencumbered. Why don't Jerry like cats? My dad always says you can't trust a man what don't like cats."

"I don't know. I think he's allergic. Anyway, he says it's cats or him. I had to farm out my mom's cat when she died. Jerry wouldn't let me keep her. We can put Cosmo in the spare bedroom. Neither one of us uses that much."

Madeleine got the bowls from the kitchen and filled one with water. They moved the operation upstairs and Cody released a tubby silver and black watermelon-striped cat from the carrier. The cat inspected the dishes and the litter box and then began to snake between Cody's legs.

"Oh, yeah, I almost forgot," said the carrier, reaching into his pocket. He withdrew a small ball of orange fuzzy material. "It's got catnip in it and he goes wild for it. That oughtta keep him occupied for a while. But I did forget something. I didn't bring the wet food and he'll make a racket over that. I can get it after we get the bundles. Meantime, a bowl of milk oughtta do the trick."

They banded and bagged the first hundred papers in relative silence. Then Cody tossed the last paper from his pile to the stack between them. He started Betty up and did a u-turn in the alley.

"You hungry?" he asked.

"Starving. I could use some coffee too," Madeleine replied. "Maybe we could go talk to Fayed, see if he's got anything new on the Spooks."

"We can catch up with Fayed later. I can stop at my dad's house and raid his fridge while I get the cat food. Won't take long."

Cody traveled though the deserted streets to an older residential section of town. He parked under an elm tree and bounded up the terraced concrete steps to the front porch of a gray frame house.

Madeleine watched him disappear into the house and sighed. She really had a craving for pancakes drowning in IHOP's syrup, chased with steaming hot coffee. Some sausage links would be great, too, and maybe a glass of OJ. He could have fed the stupid cat after they did the route. She picked up a newspaper, rolled it tight, and snapped a rubber band on it an extra round. It helped take her mind off the food and her aggravation at Cody—for what? It was only a cat, for crying out loud. It wasn't as if he'd abandoned her or their cause. It wasn't as if he'd slipped off to have "one more for the road."

The laundress shifted in her seat and her feet labored to make the necessary adjustment. Looking down at the floor, she discovered she was knee deep in a mound of paper tubes. Amazing what one could do when the mind was otherwise occupied.

Fifteen minutes later the front door opened and Cody emerged with several brown paper shopping bags. He set the bags down and locked the door behind him, pushing on it to test its security. Madeleine leaned over and opened the driver's side door, taking the bags as he climbed in. She inhaled deeply. Hot popcorn, dripping with butter and salt! What was in the other bag? She stuck her hand in and pulled out a six pack of Coca-Cola.

"Dang! This is just like going to the movies!"

Cody grabbed her hand as she was shoving it deep

50

into the bag of popcorn.

"First-off we gotta band the next two bundles," he said.

"What?! You mean I have to sit here smelling this wonderful popcorn smell and not be able to touch it until I've bagged two hundred papers? It will be totally soggy when I'm done! How could you be so mean?"

She dug her hand back in the bag and grabbed a handful of the precious corn and pelted Cody. Popcorn flew at his face. It flew at the window. It flew at the dash. He grabbed a fistful and threw it back at Madeleine, quickly following with another and another. Then Cody reached his right arm around her neck and with his left hand smeared her face in popcorn.

Madeleine was too busy laughing, chewing and trying to get into the bag for new ammunition to see the kiss coming. It was sudden and hot and thorough. And, like the popcorn, it left her wanting more.

"Um-m. A little butter, salt, and you taste just as good as I thought." Cody grinned and picked a few pieces of popcorn out of Madeleine's hair.

"Dang! This *is* just like the movies." Madeleine lifted her hand to the brim of Cody's cap and tugged hard. "I think I'm supposed to slap you now," she said and pulled his face to hers.

"If this is a slap, what does a fella hafta do to get a beating?" he murmured against her cheek.

Newspapers rustled around her feet as the two embraced. The laundress suddenly gasped.

"That good, was it?" asked Cody.

"No," she replied. "I hit my funny bone on the brake."

"We need a bigger rink to skate in," said Cody. "And *you* need to say bye-bye to Jerry."

"I know. I've just been putting it off for the past three years," Madeleine sighed. "Every time I get to the breaking point he straightens up and I get hopeful."

"Well now you have more of a reason to stick with the plan. I don't do threes."

Madeleine picked popcorn from Cody's shirt pocket and popped it into her mouth. "Best popcorn I've had in years," she said. "So why did you hit on me if you knew I live with someone and you don't do threes?"

"I been waiting a long time for you to ditch Jerry, but it weren't happening. I had to get whatcha call proactive," the carrier replied. He ate the whole kernels on his clothing and swept the crumbs to the floor.

"Now if I thought for a minute that you really wanted to be with Jerry, this wouldda been just a teaching gig."

"So you weren't using the surveillance lesson as bait?"

"Well," he drew the word out, "I hadda generate some kinda interest—and you still don't know if I'm a briefs or a boxer kinda guy."

"Or commando!" Madeleine responded and smacked him on the head with a paper.

CHAPTER 14

In the warm darkness of Madeleine's guest bedroom, Cosmo was tiring of the catnip mouse. He had chased it around the room and under the bed, batted it up in the air and rubbed it against his muzzle and whiskers to get the full sensory effect of the catnip. He had inspected every surface of the room and thoroughly snuffled all the shoes in the closet. Now it was time for his treat, but Cody had not come back. Cosmo tucked a striped paw under the door to see if the door would open. It rattled a little but did not give way. He scratched at the door lightly and then put both paws up on the door, arching his full back. He could get the paws up to the knob, but to no avail. He sat back on his haunches and thumped his tail.

Similar noises were rising from the floor below. Something scratch-scratch-scratched, and then there was a tinkling noise. The tabby waited for the sound of a metal lid being peeled from a can. There was no such noise. Instead there was a loud bump followed by a human grunt. All this noise and no treat. Cosmo began to yowl.

"Wha' the Hell? Can't a body sleep aroun' here. Madeleine!"

Thuds vibrated across the hardwood floor from the room next door. Cosmo crouched watching the human feet approach in the slice of dim light under the door. The knob rotated and the portal opened to reveal a man clad in Levis and a threadbare flannel robe. Cosmo backed up under the bed to avoid the thundering feet. At the sounds of a rusty hinge squeaking and metal sliding against metal, the tabby became hopeful. A cabinet opening was usually a good sign of treats to come. He followed the feet out into the hallway and, as they approached the stairway, he expressed his gratitude by entwining himself between the human's legs.

"Wha' the hell? Shit! Git away!" The feet tried to kick loose the cloying cat. Cosmo responded in kind. Up the pants he climbed, claws fully extended. The human emitted an ear-piercing shriek. Cosmo twisted to spring away from the legs and caught a claw in the Levis. As he struggled to free himself, the human shook its leg, batting at the tabby with the wooden end of a long metal object. Arms and paws flailed as the two overbalanced and hurtled into the stairwell.

Thump, bump, crunch, ka-boom!

Bits of plaster, lath, and fur settled on the flannel robe. A floorboard creaked and a figure appeared in the kitchen doorway. The man stared at a tail convulsing from under the heap at the bottom of the stairs. He shuddered and retreated into the kitchen. He pulled the sleeve cuff of his gray, hooded sweatshirt down over his hand, opened the kitchen door and left.

CHAPTER 15

"Mad, I need another favor," said the carrier. He stepped out of the Corolla, brushed popcorn off the seat, and removed the floor mat to shake off the crumbs.

"Favor or a beating?" asked the laundress, following suit. She was hoping for the latter.

"Later, doll. Right now I gotta to talk to the Circ' man," he replied. He checked his watch. "I need you to put the papers in at IHOP, shoot the Garth Road tubes, and meet up with me at the dock. I'll set up the tape so's you don't miss none."

"Okay," said Madeleine, "but that'll cost you a pound of flesh."

"I think I can afford that," said Cody.

As soon as Cody was safely in the building, Madeleine headed out Garth Road to fill the tubes. She didn't need the tape, but listened to it anyway, just to hear the carrier's voice. Fast forwarding past the IHOP parts, she skipped to the Garth Road cues. Madeleine hurried along the winding road, ignoring the carrier's instructions to take the curves at a slow pace. As she rounded a bend marked with a yellow safety sign recommending twenty-five mph, a small black animal with a solid white stripe down its back sauntered onto the road ahead of her. Betty screeched to a halt, but the animal paid no heed. It ambled down the center of the road at a leisurely pace of three miles per hour. Madeleine had no choice but to follow the skunk and its pungent odor. The road was flanked on either side with a deep ditch, and every time Madeleine attempted to pass to the left or to the right, the creature veered off in that direction. After a mile and a half, the skunk stopped in its tracks. Its tail shook a signature salute; then it turned off the road and disappeared down a driveway. Madeleine sped up and finished that section of the route. She turned off the tape, shut the air intake vent to block the smell, and set course for the IHOP.

The IHOP parking lot was deserted, except for the silver Lexus parked behind the building. There was no sign of the Crown Victoria, nor were there any signs of life in rooms 203 and 205.

Madeleine set the brake, grabbed the scissors from the dashboard, and pulled up the bundle marked for this address. She took ten unrolled papers and stacked them on top of the bundle. Then she squeezed out of the driver's seat onto the pavement, bumping the door shut with her fanny. It took only seconds to swap old for new papers in the newspaper box, and she calculated that she still had a few minutes to talk to Fayed. She pushed through the door into the IHOP and unloaded her burden onto the counter next to the register.

"Good morning, Miss Carrier. I've been expecting you," said the olive-skinned man behind the counter. His tongue tripped over the r's, turning them into d's.

"I am instructed to send you back to the newspaper building straight away. You must not delay! Here are yesterday's returns for Mr. Cody."

Fayed took the bundle from her arms and handed back his returns, plus the loose papers she had retrieved from the newspaper box outside the building.

"But he can wait just a minute—" Madeleine said and began to set down her load on the counter.

"No no, Miss! You must go now!" Fayed stated with no further explanation. He turned from the counter and hurried away to the kitchen.

Madeleine shrugged and left the building. She felt deflated and utterly without purpose. Why was Cody keeping her away from Fayed? She was certain that this was his intent. What did Fayed know that she wasn't supposed to know? Deep in thought, she opened the trunk and tossed in the returns. She did not notice the man in a gray hooded sweatshirt in the passenger seat until she shut the door.

"Where's your friend tonight?" asked the man from inside his hood.

Madeleine's hand stopped just short of the dash array. Her fingers curled over the scissor handles, and she lowered her hand to her lap. Maybe this was just one of those sleazy friends of Jerry's out spying on her—or maybe the Colonel and the Suits had gotten wind of her and Cody's surveillance runs. Well, now she would know. A twitch began in the arch of her foot, the kind of twitch that turned into toe tapping; she willed it to stop. Slowly she turned to face the man, trying to force the fear from her throat.

"Who are you?" she asked.

"Looks like he left you all alone to run the business." He ignored her question. "Looks to me like you need a little company." His right arm reached toward Madeleine's torso, beefy fingers splayed wide.

Madeleine made a fist and slammed it back against the intruder's thigh; the scissors pierced his pants and dug deep into the skin below. She jerked her hand back and then began to jab at the leg.

"Agh! You crazy bitch!" Her assailant shrieked and lurched at the door, one hand fending off the blows while the other fumbled with the door latch. The door opened and the man escaped into the darkness. A moment later a car started up in the parking lot of the Doubletree Hotel, but Madeleine's teeth were chattering so loudly she couldn't hear it.

"Miss! Miss!" Fayed was knocking on the driver's side window. His eyes widened as he noticed the blood stains on the passenger seat. "Oh no! You must come inside. I will call Mr. Cody."

He helped the laundress out of the car, gently pulled the scissors from her bloody fingers, and laid them on the dash. Gathering the keys, Fayed then locked the car, wrapped his arm around Madeleine and herded her in through the rear door of the restaurant.

CHAPTER 16

"I can't leave you alone for a minute, can I," said Cody, pulling up a chair in Fayed's office. "You're bound and determined to get into trouble. Now we *really* gotta find out who the Suits are, and what's going on with the Colonel's undies."

Madeleine glared at him from inside a white cocoon. Though wrapped head to red rubber toe in a tablecloth, she was still shivering. Hot cocoa sloshed from side to side in the IHOP coffee cup. She set the cup down. Her hands were clean but still felt blood-sticky.

"It's not like I invited him to get in the car. Why are you treating me as if *I* started this? I never even saw him 'til I was in the car. He was already in there. He knew it was your car and you weren't with me. He was watching us. We were watching the 'Suits,' and he was watching us."

"You're sure all you said to him was 'Who are you?'" Cody asked. He pulled the chair closer to the laundress, reached for the cup, and took a sip.

"How many times do I have to say it? Yes, that's all I said." Tears began to stream down Madeleine's cheeks; she rolled her head across her shoulder to blot them.

Cody pulled Madeleine's hand from the cocoon and cradled it between his own. Her fingers were dry and rough from years of working in detergent and bleach. He opened the palm and stroked it with his thumb.

"Whadda you think?" he asked, looking up at Fayed, who was standing in the doorway. The Pakistani stepped inside and shut the door.

"One thing is certain," he replied, "he will not be going to the authorities. If he goes to hospital, they must file a police report, so I don't think he will go there either.

He will have to have the wounds bound by a confederate."

"And I wonder who that could be. It ain't the Suits. That blood trail ends in the lot here. The tire tread ain't right for a Crown Vic. Maybe it's time to call the cops. It'll seem weird if we don't call them."

"It will most definitely, and there is no need to call attention," said Fayed. He moved to a spot behind Madeleine and leaned back against a bookshelf. "Perhaps it is also time to install a security camera."

"I like the ole way myself, but I can see your point," mused Cody. "The neighborhood is gettin' a little dicey, and you're open all hours. The company'll probably spot you for it.

"Well Ms. Mummy, are you ready?"

"As ready as I'll ever be," replied Madeleine. She pulled the table cloth off of her head and repositioned herself in the chair.

Cody stood up. He leaned over and plucked a piece of popcorn from Madeleine's tousled hair.

"I wonder if he ate any popcorn while he was waitin' for you. That could be some evidence for the cops. He's bound to have it on him." Cody smiled. He reached out his arms, laced his fingers and turned them backwards and giving his knuckles a loud crack. "Good."

CHAPTER 17

"I guess this guy was getting a volume discount on his Old Milwaukee. There must be three or four cases of empties by the back door." Detective James Knight squatted down and rifled through the broken glass on the floor with his pocket knife.

"There's a few spots of blood here, Rick. Hey, Mitch, bring your camera over here and get some shots of this. Let's send some slides down to the lab too, and see if we get a match anywhere."

He stood up and picked his way carefully across the kitchen floor. Wandering through the living room, he lifted, examined and replaced items on the coffee table, couch and mantle. He picked up an unframed team photograph of a women's softball league and looked for familiar faces. The officer peered at the photo from over his shoulder.

"I've seen that one before. She's the one who was running papers with Cody the other night when we had Alderman blocked off."

"Yeah, here she is with Mr. Milwaukee," replied Detective Knight, pointing to a silver framed four-by-six photograph on the mantle. "I wonder if she's running route with Cody tonight. There are two cars in the driveway, so he may have picked her up here. Why don't you talk to the neighbor and see if she saw anyone come or go earlier tonight."

He turned toward the stairs and stopped. On the stairs an enormous silver tabby cat was perched on top of the dead man's stomach. He was busily engaged in cleaning his nether regions, one hind leg extended. Detective Knight reached over and picked up the cat. He scratched it under its chin and behind the ears.

"If only you could talk, fella. I'll bet you saw it all. Well, you're going to have to sit this one out for a while. You'll just mess up my crime scene if you stay here. I know I saw a carrier somewhere. Let's see if we can find it. And if you're lucky maybe someone will come up with some tuna."

"Yeow," replied Cosmo.

CHAPTER 18

"Ma'am, what time did you leave your house tonight?" asked the officer. He pushed his glasses up on the bridge of his nose, flipped a page in his spiral note pad and began to jot down notes.

"About one-thirty or so. Cody picked me up to do the newspaper route. We stopped to roll papers for a while and then we went to his dad's house. He fixed us a snack and . . ." Madeleine's right toe began to tap the desk leg. The officer continued to make notes, apparently oblivious to the tapping. His glasses began to slide slightly as his head bobbed.

"We ate the snack in the car and came back to the newspaper building. Cody had some business there and so I took the next part of the route."

"And what time did you leave the newspaper office?"

"I don't know," said Madeleine. "I just dropped him off and did what he asked me to do." Her foot tapped faster as she remembered that she hadn't done exactly as Cody had instructed.

She added, "We don't have a time clock, except you have to have it all delivered by six-thirty."

The officer looked up from his notes and pushed the glasses back up his nose. "And was there anything different tonight about the route?"

Madeleine was confused. Which thing did he want to know: about the man in the car, about the order of the route, or was it about her and Cody? She decided she was being paranoid, and it was nobody's business but their own anyway. Never volunteer anything. Wasn't that what Cody always said? She wished he was with her, not in the dining area having coffee with the other officer.

"No sir, unless you count the skunk."

"Skunk?"

"There was a skunk on Garth Road and I got stuck behind it for a couple miles. It sprayed the car," she replied.

"So, you don't know what time you got to the newspaper office or what time it was when you arrived at the IHOP. When did you discover that there was someone in your vehicle?"

"I dropped the bundles and got the returns from the IHOP manager, so it was when I got back in the car to pick up Cody."

"Was the car locked or unlocked when you went into the restaurant?"

"I was only in there a minute," Madeleine defended herself.

"So it was unlocked," said the officer, and flipped another page in his notebook. "What happened next?"

"The guy asked me where Cody was and said it looked like I needed company. I asked him who he was. No. I asked him who he was and then he said it looked like I needed company. Then he reached out like he was going to grab me, so I stuck him in the leg with the scissors." Madeleine's heart began to pound again as she recalled the hand coming toward her.

"There was a lot of blood on the passenger seat," remarked the officer, looking up from his notating. "Did you strike him more than once?"

"What do you mean, did I strike him more than once? Of course I did. He wasn't getting the hell out of the car!" her voice rose to fever pitch.

The officer made a note and asked, "Did you make any attempt to get out of the vehicle yourself?"

Madeleine stared at him. It had never occurred to her to get out of the car. Why didn't she do that? Why did she keep jabbing him until he had jumped out of the car?

"No," she replied.

"Describe his appearance," said the officer.

"Before or after I stuck him? I never saw his face," said the laundress, "but I'd know his voice if I ever heard it again."

"What was he wearing?"

"Jeans and a gray sweatshirt. He had the hood up so I couldn't see his face. Then he got out of the car and I didn't see where he went."

"Did he ever actually physically touch you?" asked the officer. He removed his glasses, rubbed the bridge of his nose with his thumb and middle fingers, and then replaced the glasses.

"Did he ever actually physically touch you?" repeated the officer.

"No," said Madeleine.

The officer shut his notebook and slid it and the pen into his breast pocket. "I guess that about wraps it up here. We'll need you to come downtown and make an official statement."

"Wasn't this making a statement? Why do I have to do it all again?" asked Madeleine. "We have a route to finish. Can't I do this tomorrow? You have all the information I can give you. Shouldn't you be out there looking for the guy?"

"Ma'am, it's all procedure. You'll have to come with us." He punched the tiny radio clipped to his shoulder and spoke something indecipherable into it. Seconds later his partner opened Fayed's office door and stepped inside.

"We got pics and samples already. They've all gone ahead. You done here?"

"I believe so." Rising to his full six-foot three-inch height, the officer straightened his glasses at the temples and shoved them back up the bridge of his nose. He turned to Madeleine. "Shall we?"

CHAPTER 19

Detective Knight reviewed the officer's notes and handed the notebook back. Something wasn't adding up here. On the surface all the events matched, but he could smell a lie. What were the odds on a burglary and a death at this woman's house on the same night that she was assaulted at the IHOP? He had deliberately withheld any information about the events at her house, hoping she would tip her hand. So far her story had not deviated. Nor had Cody's. Maybe it was time to shift tactics.

"So, Ms. Dresser—"

"That's Dreiser, like an eye," Madeleine said, and pointed at her right eye.

"Ms. Dreiser," he resumed, "have you contacted anyone at home tonight?" The detective leaned back in the metal chair.

"At home? No." It occurred to Madeleine that she hadn't given Jerry the first thought since going into the IHOP. No, that wasn't true. She had thought about the irony of her situation, how Jerry had obsessed over her safety and how she might be "doing the newspaper guy," as he had termed it. All his worst fears were being realized.

"Ms. Dreiser, would you like to call someone?"

"Does this mean I can go now?"

"You didn't answer my question. Would you like to call someone?"

Madeleine also smelled a lie. To her it was a giant hole where information should be. That same kind of hole had inspired her to investigate the Suits. She wondered if the police had somehow gotten wind of her surveillance project. She wondered what Cody had told them. There were too many "what ifs" to know how to proceed. It was better to err on the side of caution.

"There's no point in calling home. Jerry was passed out drunk when Cody picked me up for the route. He'll be that way until noon. He couldn't drive even if I did wake him up."

"Was Jerry drunk or was he in fact dead when you left your house this morning, Ms. Dreiser?"

"Dead? Of course not. Why would you—" Her voice trailed off.

Madeleine began to glimpse the enormity of the pit before her. The Suits must have killed Jerry to warn her off. What else would they do to stop her interference? An acrid smell rose from her armpits and perspiration tickled down the inside of her upper right arm. She leaned forward and hooked her toes around the chair legs to still them.

"Oh, God. What happened?"

"At approximately two o'clock this morning officers responded to a call reporting screams and a gunshot coming from your house. There was evidence of a break-in, and the other occupant of your house—your boyfriend, I believe?—was lying on the stairs dead with a broken neck. Witnesses reported a man in a hooded sweatshirt in the neighborhood at that time. Looks pretty simple on the surface. But then there's this other call an hour later about an assault on you at the IHOP, where the actual injured party is a man in a hooded sweatshirt.

"Oh, did I mention the blood on the kitchen floor at your house where the alleged burglar entered? I think we'll find it matches the blood in the car. I think you know who the man in the hooded sweatshirt is. No more games, Ms. Dreiser. I want his name *now*." The detective slammed his palm on the table and Madeleine jumped.

"I don't know his name! I never saw him before!" the laundress retorted. "I can't give you what I don't have. That man was going to hurt me. He would have hurt me if I hadn't stuck him with those scissors, and I'm not sorry I stuck him. Maybe you should find him and ask *him* why he broke into my house and then showed up at the IHOP just when I was delivering the papers there. I wasn't in my own car and I wasn't even doing the route in the order I was supposed to."

"And why was that, Ms. Dreiser? Why did you change the delivery order?" asked the detective. He drummed his index and middle fingers on the table and waited for the lie.

"Because I'm an idiot," said Madeleine, and meant it. "It was the first time I did any of the route on my own. There's a tape you listen to, and I punched fast forward instead of play. I figured I could go back to the IHOP later, and that's what I did. I didn't know anything about Jerry at home. I had no way to know what happened."

Detective Knight studied the woman before him. Without the lab results he had little to go on, but he could still feel the presence of a lie. She didn't show the emotion of loss, only anger. He went fishing.

"Your boyfriend was a drunk. Maybe it was a convenient end to a miserable relationship. Maybe Mr. Hooded Sweatshirt was a new beau who was only supposed to scare him into leaving. Maybe the fall down the stairs was accidental. Maybe you and Mr. Hooded Sweatshirt had it out when you learned that Jerry was dead."

"I *told* you I didn't know anything about Jerry 'til you brought it up just now. The house is mine. If I was ready to call it quits, I would just tell Jerry to leave. I wouldn't need somebody else to do it for me." She folded her arms across her bosom and leaned back.

The door opened and an officer poked his head through the opening. "Detective, you got a minute?"

Detective Knight stood up and walked to the door. He turned halfway and spoke to the laundress, "We both know you are withholding evidence, Ms. Dreiser. When I come back we can discuss the penalties for withholding evidence, and perhaps you will change your mind."

On the other side of the door Detective Knight's assistant Rick was watching Madeleine through the two-way mirror. Her arms remained folded across her chest, but she had pulled her right foot across her knee and the red-rubber toe was tapping empty air.

"What do you have?" asked Detective Knight.

"She's telling the truth."

"About what?"

"She actually *was* running the route where and when she said she was. I confirmed it with some of the other carriers who have run that route. Actually it was the skunk that nailed it."

"The skunk," repeated Detective Knight.

"Yes, sir." He cleared his throat and elaborated. "Apparently skunks are very habitual and this one travels on Garth Road every night at the same time, between one forty-five and two AM. Because of that none of the other carriers want this stretch of road. So Cody gets it, even though he has hardly any other customers in that vicinity. Cody says he made the tape with instructions that put you on the road after the skunk has passed. I checked out the tape, and that's correct. Do you want to review it yourself?"

"No, that won't be necessary. Just make a copy of it for the file.

"Anything back from the lab yet?" He picked a cat hair off the lapel of his jacket.

"Time of death estimated at one-thirty to two o'clock. The lab confirms that the front grille of the car was sprayed by a skunk."

"Rick, blood results?"

"Oh yeah. The blood in the Toyota matches the blood in the house. AB-Negative. Not too many people with that type; it's the rarest one. I already checked the hospitals. Nobody's been in tonight with that blood type."

"Nose around a bit and see what you can dig up on Ms. Dreiser," said Detective Knight. He rubbed a muscle at the back of his neck and then rolled his head around from left to right and back. "The blood match is good but I need something more. She may have been behind the skunk but I'm not buying the part where she doesn't know anything about the sweatshirt guy. She knows something."

"What about Cody?"

"Cody? I don't think there's anything there. He was at the newspaper office with the circulation manager. He's alibied to the hilt. They both heard the B&E report across the scanner. He got a ride to the IHOP with Potter."

"Potter?"

"I forgot. He's before your time. Potter used to work vice for the County. Has his own gig now. He was the biggest pain in the ass—used to waste my time with those stories.

"Speaking of which, go ahead and release them, but keep an eye on her. Better yet, why don't you suggest that Cody take her to id the body and keep an eye on her. Then we can put one man on the both of them."

"That's putting the wolf in the hen house, isn't it?"

Detective Knight looked through the glass and smiled. "Oh, she's a big girl. I think she'll do just fine."

CHAPTER 20

Madeleine lay fully clothed, but shoeless, on her right side on the queen-sized bed, facing away from the open bedroom door. A dim light from the bathroom illuminated the red rubber-toed sneakers sitting side-by-side on the floor next to the bed. Cosmo was curled up against her tummy and purring loudly. Claws retracted, his paws gently kneaded her thigh. It was comforting and she accepted it as a gift from a compatriot. They had both been through hell tonight.

The laundress shut her eyes but images from the morgue, the house and the car continued to dart across her eyelids. She opened them and sighed. Sleep apparently was not an option.

"Here's a little something to take the edge off." Cody offered Madeleine a mug of steaming cocoa. He moved Cosmo's tail and sat down on the bed next to them.

"I can't, not now," she said, setting the mug on the bedside table.

"Havin' trouble with what you saw at the morgue?"

She nodded and rubbed Cosmo behind the ears. "And the house. God, what a mess. Holes in the ceiling. Plaster and lath everywhere. It'll take me weeks to clean up all that fingerprint dust they left.

"Jerry was a drunk, but he didn't deserve this. I'm going to get those Suits if it's the last thing I do." Madeleine rubbed a little too vigorously on a tender spot, and Cosmo extended a single warning claw into her thigh. "Ouch!"

"Come on, boy," said Cody. He lifted the tabby onto his lap and shifted into the warm space beside Madeleine.

"You know, Mad, the Suits aren't the ones who did this."

"Okay, so the tire tread isn't from a Crown Victoria, but they could have gotten somebody else to do it for them," said Madeleine. She pushed the pillow upward with her elbow and sat up against it.

"That was skinny tread, a small car, and the tread weren't new. The Suits wouldda hired somebody professional, not a hack."

Madeleine reached for the mug and sucked off the skin that was developing on the cocoa. She licked her lips. The cocoa was as good as the popcorn. She sipped some more and reflected on the day's events.

"Did you tell the police about the Suits?" she asked.

"Nope. Did you?"

"No," she exhaled. "I didn't know what to say, so I didn't say anything."

"Good," said Cody.

"The detective accused me of withholding evidence. He said there were penalties. Can I go to jail because I didn't tell him about the Suits?"

"Did you answer his questions?"

She nodded.

"Did you tell him anything that weren't true?"

She shook her head.

"Then you're good."

"But—"

"No buts. You don't *know* that the Suits are up to anything. All you got is a piece of something on a computer, and that's about a colonel's skivvies. You wanna tell that to the detective? Nah. You did good."

"Well, thanks for that vote of confidence." She set the mug down.

"So, Cody, when were you planning to tell me about Jerry?" Madeleine asked. She leaned back against the pillow, arms folded across her bosom, and crossed her feet.

Cody moved Cosmo back to the bed and stood up. He pulled his T-shirt over his head and tossed it on an Ottoman at the foot of the bed. He circled around the bed toward the bathroom and stopped in front of a tall chest of drawers. There he removed his wrist watch and laid it on the chest.

Madeleine stared at his silhouette as she waited for an answer. Even in the poor light she could see that he had not one ounce of fat on his body. His muscles, though well-defined, were not those of a body builder. His jeans rode low on the hips and tight across the buttocks. Commando? She almost forgot her question.

"They got a police scanner goin' twenty-four/seven at the office. I called the IHOP when I heard the dispatcher give your 'twenty'—that's address in cop lingo," Cody addressed her via a mirror mounted on a three-drawer box on the chest. "Fayed said you hadn't got there yet, so I told him to send you straight back to the office whenever you showed up. If you'd a done like I asked, it wouldda took fifteen minutes. It was a full hour before Fayed called to tell me about the guy you carved up in old Betty."

"It was the skunk that held me up," said Madeleine. "I couldn't get past him. And then the damned thing sprayed the car."

"Betty'll survive the skunk. I don't know about your seat. Might need crime scene clean-up folks for that," he mused as he took a comb from the box and ran it through his hair. "Anyway, you already had enough on your plate, doll. No need to muddy the waters."

"What did the circulation manager say about Bob working your territory?" She drained the mug and yawned.

"Now *that* was interesting," answered the carrier. "Seems that Bob an' Ellen didn't get the Orchard when it opened. He's tryin' to snake my territory. I guess he figures if he can get more tubes than me, Circ Man'll just give him the sub. I got news for him: Circ Man don't like snakes any more than I do."

The carrier watched Madeleine through the mirror. She had sunk down into the pillow and was snoring lightly. Cosmo was busy kneading dough on her chest.

Cody chuckled. "Some cats got all the luck."

He crossed the room took the mug from her hand and set it on the table. She mumbled something incoherent and rolled to her side, sending a disgruntled Cosmo tumbling onto her shoes. Cody opened the closet and pulled a blanket off the shelf. He unfolded it and laid it across the sleeping woman.

It took less than five minutes to do a perimeter check and re-arm the new alarm system. A shaft of sunlight shone through one curtain in the living room. He pulled the edges of the curtain together to overlap, and the shaft disappeared, leaving him in total darkness. He sat down on the couch and picked up a phone from the end table beside him.

"Hey, Dad. It's me. Yeah, I'm at the house. I brought a visitor tonight. Remember the laundromat girl I told you about? Yep, that's the one. She sure knows how to stir up some shit." His lips curved into a grin.

"Things were cookin' along pretty good and . . . yeah, *had* a boyfriend. He's dead. Nah, didn't have to." The carrier leaned back into the couch cushions and propped his right foot up on the coffee table. He wagged his foot and head from side to side in unison as he listened.

"Anyway, I think we're up to the hip in something here. I don't know what but it ain't good. Yeah. I'll keep you posted. I think she might be here a few days.

"Oh, I re-did the alarm, and it's not quite finished. So don't just come traipsing in without telling me, okay? Yeah. You too."

He dropped the receiver back onto the cradle. He wondered what the stake-out was having for breakfast. He'd noticed the lone, white, American-made sedan parked down the block when he shut the curtain. It sported standard government plates and a search light mounted on the driver's side fender.

Cody pulled a fleece throw off the opposite arm of the couch and wrapped it around himself. He repositioned an accent pillow for his head and swung his legs onto the couch.

"Morons," he muttered, and went to sleep.

CHAPTER 21

"I'm sorry for your loss, Ma'am," said the customer as Madeleine handed him a roll of quarters for his ten.

"Bad news travels fast, doesn't it," replied Madeleine.

The man's freckled face blushed vivid red into his mop of copper red hair. "Indeed," he said and began to turn away from her.

"I'm sorry. That was a kind thing you said, and I wasn't nice. You've been coming here for six weeks and I sure don't mean to offend you with my bad attitude."

"No offense taken. Where I come from your response would have been the norm. One just doesn't expect it in the South."

"And where *are* you from?" she asked.

"New York City," he replied. "My friend and I are returning there next week. This is our last visit to your establishment . . . but not because of you."

"Why leave so soon?" she asked. "Was this just a business trip?"

"We're with a show and tonight's our last performance. Tomorrow we're off to DC and the Kennedy Center."

"Are you actors?" Madeleine asked, eager to say she knew one.

"No, we're production . . . costuming actually." He set the roll down on the counter and dug into his hip pocket. He pulled a card out and handed it to Madeleine.

"Here's a comp ticket to the show if you'd like to go. Maybe it would help get your mind off all the crap you're going through."

Madeleine turned the card over and read it. She was unfamiliar with the play, but the idea struck a chord. It had

79

been several years since she'd seen a live production of
anything, and she needed to do something for herself.
There was no more Jerry to ride her about going out, so
why the hell not go? "Okay," she said. "I'll go. Thanks a lot
. . . and break an arm."

"You mean, 'break a leg'," he said.

"Yeah, break a leg. Just don't break your neck," she
said and laughed for the first time since popcorn.

The laundress returned to the routine tasks of the
day: wiping down counter space, running the dust mop
over the floor, wiping off washers and doing the requisite
hundred pounds of drop-off. Bags and baskets of dirty
laundry lined the floor in front of the counter, awaiting her
attention. Rita had worked Friday morning, as planned, and
then had locked the doors, with a scrawled note "Closed
Due To Death In Family" taped to the glass. The regular
customers just left their containers in front of the door
with their names attached.

Though she knew there was no hurry to get the
drop-off done, Madeleine threw herself into the task with
uncharacteristic vigor. It kept her from obsessing about the
previous day's events. The police had no new leads on the
burglar, nor were they hounding her for additional
information. They said the investigation was "ongoing," but
wouldn't divulge anything further.

Cody had found a twenty year-old punk rocker with
spiked blue and pink hair to clean the house, and Jerry's
sisters were at the house making the funeral arrangements.
Janey, the elder and more officious of the two, had taken
the helm and was directing everyone within eyesight. Her
jet black hair was pulled away from a wasp-like face and
tied up tightly in a French twist at the back of her head, not
a hair out of place as her head swiveled. Pick up this. Move
that. Where is Daddy's shot gun? Evidence, my foot; get it
back!

Madeleine had fled to the laundromat and now
visualized the sisters poring over her household

furnishings, divvying up everything they believed to be Jerry's. She wondered if there would be anything of any value left and she prayed that they would take Jerry's recliner and sofa. The stench of beer in them was so strong that even the Salvation Army had refused to take them when Madeleine had thrown Jerry out the last time.

A machine whooshed and clicked, signaling the end of the extract cycle on the load of darks. Madeleine pulled up the lid on the washer and pulled out a pair of black jeans and some T-shirts. At the bottom of the washer tub something rattled. She shoved the clothes into the dryer, and reached back into the washer for the rattling item. It was a six-inch opaque black plastic cylinder with a plastic base and a stem jutting from its side, a smoking device commonly known among young and aging hippies as a "bong." She fished in the washer again and removed a half-inch brass bowl, threaded at the bottom. She screwed it onto the stem and set it on the counter. There was a small plastic baggie stuffed in the center of the cylinder. The laundress pulled it out and inspected the contents. Pot, sticky, wet, and soon to be moldy. Rolling the baggie up, she stuck her tongue out to lick and stick the flap. Bag in mid-air, Madeleine thought better of the idea and replaced it in the cylinder as it was. Who knew where that man's tongue had been, even if the bag had been washed. She squatted down and rooted through the bottles of bleach, spot-removers, and fabric softener under the counter. Deep in the recesses of the cubby was a pile of paper bags. She groaned as she stretched into the space to get a bag.

"Takin' up a new hobby?" said a voice above her.

Madeleine backed out of the cubby, whacking the top of her head along the way. She rubbed her head and set the bag down on the counter.

"Damn it, Cody! Stop sneaking up on me like that! Don't you ever sleep?"

He pointed at the bong on the counter. "You know, that stuff is illegal in every state of the union. I don't think it matters if it's clean or not."

The laundress continued to rub her head with her left hand as she opened the paper bag and dropped the bong into it with her right. She stowed it under the counter, pulled the stool up and sat down. Her head throbbed and a goose egg was rising on the top.

"You okay? I could kiss it and make it better," he said, and leaned over to make good on the offer.

"I'd be more impressed if you got me an ice pack from the fridge . . . please," she replied. Putting her elbows on the counter she cradled her head in her hands and felt the contours of the growing lump.

Cody slid a flat plastic gel-filled wrap underneath her fingers. The wrap was cool at first and then turned to biting cold. Madeleine jerked it off.

"I don't know which is worse—the throbbing or the ice pack," she said, slinging the wrap onto the counter.

"A bag of frozen peas is the best thing, if you got 'em," Cody said.

He walked around the counter and stood behind Madeleine. Gently he pulled her fingers away from her head and began massaging her neck up into the scalp. The laundress's head drooped a little, then she heaved a sigh and dropped her chin to her chest. He brought his right arm around to stabilize the head against his torso and massaged from the left temple area toward the goose egg. Madeleine winced, so he reversed arms and came up from the opposite side. Cody then leaned her forward and massaged straight up from the occipital ridge through her mane to the edge of the lump and then replaced the ice pack.

"I think you missed your calling. You should be a masseuse. I'd be your best client," said Madeleine, catching the ice pack as it started to slide off.

"They call 'em 'massage therapists' now. You'd be the only client."

"Hmm," Madeleine said, relaxing into his chest. The

muscles of his torso and abdomen were taut but his arms held her with a light grip. "I was beginning to wonder if something changed. You've let me stay at your dad's house with you, and you haven't made the first move on me."

"And I probably shouldn't be doin' this either," he whispered into her left ear. "Did it ever occur to you that they're watchin' us?"

"What?" The ice pack slapped onto the counter as her head popped up. She turned around to look at the carrier. There was just the barest hint of a smile at the corners of his mouth. Her hair, wild with static electricity, was wafting out to the side, creating a half-halo. His left arm reached past her and retrieved the ice pack. He tucked errant strands of her brunette mane behind her ears and re-covered the goose egg.

"Think about it," he said. "Are they tellin' you anything new on the case? Nah. What kinda evidence do they got? One girl, two guys, one of the guys is dead and the other's carved up. It don' look good. They're waitin' to see whatcha do next.

"Knight's sidekick actually tried to buffalo me into keeping you at my place. Said he was afraid for your safety. Buncha bullshit. He just wants to make it an easy stake-out. I told him you could stay at my dad's and take care of the cat. That wasn't good enough, so I said okay, I'll sleep on the couch, like it was a pain in the ass. 'Please don' throw me in the briar patch!' Cody mimicked Brer Rabbit.

"Now, on to more important stuff. Did the Suits ever pick up their dry cleaning?" The carrier didn't wait for an answer. He went to the rack and rifled through the hangers until he found the navy three-piece suit and yellow silk tie. He inspected the label. "Damn! That's a three hundred dollar suit, and the tie ain't cheap neither," said Cody. "Who *is* this guy?" He read the ticket stapled to the hanger bag above the shoulder. "Sorkin. The name's Jewish, from Saren or Sarin, derivative of Sarah, outa Belarus."

"How do you know that?" asked Madeleine.

"It's a hobby, where people come from, migration patterns. There's a lot in a name. For instance, everybody knows that O' and Mac mean 'of the house of,' but "Ap" means the same thing in Welsh. So the name Powell comes from Ap Howell and means 'of the house of Howell.' Howells came out of Wales with the Tudors. They were foresters. Lotta names are about occupation: smith, carter, wright, maker.

"Jewish names go back thousands of years. Every time you put on a pair of Levi's, you're puttin' on a name that goes back to one of the twelve tribes of Israel. That tribe was supposed to be priests.

"This guy's family is probably second or third generation, depending on if they left Europe during the Holocaust or one of the earlier pogroms." Cody reached under the plastic bag and fingered the tie. "What's his buddy's name?"

"Scardino. Sounds Italian to me. Maybe they're Mafia," said Madeleine. "Actually, we have a lot of new drop-off customers who have Italian-sounding names. Look at the log."

She pulled the three-ring notebook across the counter toward Cody. He leaned over her shoulder and thumbed through a few pages. "First they're spies, now they're Mafia. All right, there's a lot of Italian here, but that don't prove nothin.'"

"Some of them have the same phone number. Maybe they're family—you know, like the Cosa Nostra," offered Madeleine. The gel pack was beginning to sweat, sending droplets flying every time she moved her head. When one dribbled down her nose, she snatched the pack from her head and flung it back onto the counter.

"Did ya ever call any of the numbers or look the names up in the phone book?" asked the carrier.

"No. They always pick up on time," said Madeleine.

"Well, if you had, you'da got the front desk of the

Super 8 Motel for these three, and the front desk of the Omni Hotel for these here." He pointed to each set of entries in the log.

"Doll, you need to do yer homework before you start assuming stuff. Whatever it is they do, these guys at the Super 8 are either on a low budget or they're really thrifty. The others got plenty of disposable income or they work for somebody with a big budget. Once you pair that with the clothes and the habits, you got something to start with, and I mean 'start', not 'run'.

"Come on." He reached his arm around her shoulders and gave Madeleine a squeeze. "Let's get the hell outa here. The customers have cleared out, an' the drop-off will keep."

Madeleine put the gel pack back in the freezer and got her keys. She checked her pocket for her wallet and pulled out the comp ticket. Waiving it under Cody's nose, she announced, "I'm going to the thea-tah."

"Sounds wonderful, dahling. I'm going beddie-bye," replied Cody, and he flipped the "Closed" sign around.

CHAPTER 22

Under the voluminous bed sheet Madeleine stretched her legs and pointed her toes. She smacked her toes together and then pushed her heels downward to stretch out the Achilles tendons. Steam wafted from the bathroom where Cody was showering. She wondered what he looked like naked and imagined taking a peek. The water stopped and she rolled to her side, back to the door, so as not to appear too eager. Madeleine's remorse over Jerry and her desire for Cody seemed to inflame each other. She decided not to be the one to make the first advance.

To her dismay, the carrier came through the room without stopping. She heard one or two creaks as he moved about downstairs, and then he was back in the bedroom. He set a glass of water on the bedside table and headed into the bathroom. When he returned he propped a couple of pillows against the headboard and sat up against them. The scent of Irish Spring drifted up her nose and Madeleine's heart began to thump. His white terry cloth sleeve rustled as he touched the pulse point below her ear.

"Well, you're not asleep. Let's see how that egg is doin.'" Cody turned on his side, and with his left hand began massaging in slow, rounded strokes from the base of the neck to the edge of the lump. He traced a line around the lump and then moved his long fingers past her ear to the pulse point. He nuzzled the nape of her neck. "Definitely not asleep."

Cody pulled the covers down to Madeleine's elbow, reached across her hip and laced his fingers through hers. He traced the contours of her face and throat. Damp curls brushed against her as he kissed her ear. He tightened his elbow and closed the gap between them.

"You lead and I'll follow," he whispered and

squeezed her fingers slightly. Their fingers moved in tandem across her night shirt, dipping deep into the V-neckline. Fire seared a path from her right breast to the wet space between her legs. Madeleine could stand it no longer. She freed her hand and turned her body to face Cody. His azure eyes held hers as she jerked the covers away and pulled at the terry robe tie.

"Commando!" she breathed.

"Ah ah ah," he said in a mock warning. He pulled the night shirt over her head in one motion. "Tit for tat," he said, exploring her olive breasts with his hands and lips.

Madeleine ran her fingers through Cody's curls and inhaled his scent. She tugged and brought his mouth to hers. He tasted of sweet corn as his tongue met hers. She ran her fingers from the base of his spine straight up to his neck, and felt him come to attention against her abdomen.

"Tut tut. Feels like rain," said Cody as he fished in a robe pocket. "You have about 10 seconds to stop that or I won't be held accountable," he added and slipped her panties off.

"Damn! You are one quick study," Madeleine gasped as he touched her favorite spots with unerring precision. He drew her left knee up and pressed gently against the slippery opening. A surge of electricity rippled through her body and out through her toes. Cody rocked her with slow rhythmic movements as she caught her breath and the fire inside her resumed. Beads of sweat broke out on his forehead but he kept their gaze locked. One after the other they convulsed, panting, and collapsed onto the bed.

From behind them there came a scratching noise. Madeleine craned her neck to hear it. The next noise was indisputable.

"Ye-ow!" wailed a voice on the other side of the bedroom door.

"Talk about a mood-breaker. Well, at least he

waited until the end of Round One. Cosmo hates bein' left out," said Cody. He hadn't changed positions but things were re-arranging themselves, so he tidied up and let the cat inside. Cosmo sniffed the sheets briefly and then tucked himself next to Madeleine's tummy. Madeleine rubbed Cosmo's chin and the cat began to purr and knead her thigh.

"That was pretty spectacular. What do you do for an encore?" she asked.

"Oh, I can do a lot better than that," he answered, sliding back into bed. "You been outa circalation too long, that's all."

"What do you mean?"

"Well, most women just take a long time—you know . . . too much junk in their heads or something. You, you got right down to business, and you got one hell of a vice grip in there, doll. You can't fake that." He laughed and rolled to the opposite side of the bed to avoid being kicked.

"You wanted a nap and a shower before going to the theater gig. You might wanna take the shower now," Cody suggested.

Madeleine looked down at the kitty curled up beside her. "Good idea," she replied.

CHAPTER 23

The streets were dark but not empty as Madeleine drove toward Culbreth Theatre. Oak trees swayed in a light wind, their leaves flying like starlings in envelope formations. Leaves and road debris danced in the glare of oncoming headlights. The laundress rolled down the window a little and breathed in the cool September air.

Madeleine was spruced up in khaki pants, an off-white, button-up shirt and dark green vest. The hard leather of her penny loafers slid around on the pedals until she made the adjustment from sneakers to shoes. Dressing up was not Madeleine's strong suit, and, short of the newly purchased funeral attire, this was as good as it got.

An exhilarating rush traveled through her body as she recalled Round Two in the shower. Cody had redefined the uses of a bar of soap. He had also demonstrated the value of a portable shower bench. It was not just for seniors anymore. Her toes twitched as she considered the alternative uses of a hand-held shower head with an extra-long hose.

Block after block fell away while the laundress contemplated the past week. Somehow she had gone from one boyfriend to two and then back to one, from a passing acquaintance to a hot romance. It struck her that she didn't even know Cody's last name. How on earth could she have slept with a man whose name she didn't know?

And then there was this one trivial item that didn't seem to fit—commando. How could Cody be such a neatnik and yet go commando? He didn't seem the biker type, nor did he fit the hippie type. She might not have considered it thus, but for the fact that she had ridden with him on his route and seen that dash array. He was also spotless at his father's house. Everything seemed to have a place and he always took care to put things back when not in use. The images conveyed vastly different personality types to the laundress. Which was he?

The traffic light changed and a horn honked behind Madeleine. Autopilot had brought her to the intersection by the laundromat, so she rounded the corner and pulled into the parking lot to make a U-turn. The laundress was almost out of the lot when, in the rear view mirror, she spotted a paper tacked to the door. She moved the stick to neutral, pulled up the brake and hopped out.

"URGENT!! WE NEED TO PICK UP THE DRY CLEANING. PLEASE CALL ASAP!! SCARDINO" was written in large block letters on a half piece of spiral notebook paper. Madeleine looked at the clock through the door glass. If she hustled she could deliver the dry cleaning to the DoubleTree and still make the play on time. She grabbed the keys from the ignition, and tried to block the thoughts about letting the Suits get away. Maybe, if she played her cards right, she could still pull a rabbit out of the hat.

The clerk at the DoubleTree was extremely annoyed at the intrusion. In the back room Alex Trebek was delivering answers to a Jeopardy panel, answers to which the clerk knew the appropriate questions. His gaze kept darting back toward the room with the television between rapid-fire dialing Rooms 203 and 205. There was no response. He shrugged and suggested she try again later. Madeleine felt in her pocket for the note as proof, but found only a twenty dollar bill. In her haste she had left the note behind.

"Could I leave it here for them?" she asked. "I don't have time to go back to the shop."

"Lady, we don't have room for things like that. No closets, no hooks. Sorry," he replied and turned to the rear.

"Well, could you unlock the door and let me leave it in one of the rooms?" she begged.

"No, ma'am. I can't leave the front."

"Look," said Madeleine, "they left a note saying it

was urgent that they get it back. I've had a death in the family and I don't know when I'm going to be open again for them to pick it up. It's an expensive suit, so it must be a big occasion." She dug her fingers into her pockets and leaned across the counter with the twenty. "How about if you just give me the key and let me go do it myself. Then everybody will be happy and you can go back to your game. Please?"

"Well—okay," said the clerk. "Don't ever tell anyone I let you do it though. They fire people for less here."

"Thank you, thank you!" Madeleine squeezed his hand between both of hers and palmed off the twenty.

The closet of Room 205 held a few polo shirts, some button ups and two sweaters. Madeleine was familiar with all of these, and found one of her drop-off bags on the floor of the closet, crammed with soiled clothing. Again, they were items denoting a variety of pursuits, from painting to white collar business.

She looked around the room. The laptop was on the table by the window. How did those things work? She felt around the edges for a latch or a power switch. While the machine booted up, Madeleine looked around for floppy disks. Most people kept the disks with the computer unless there was a security risk. The laptop made a hoarse squeak, indicating "ready" mode.

In the hallway outside, the elevator dinged and Madeleine froze. The voices were unmistakable: the Suits. The laundress slapped the top down and looked around the room for a place to hide. The closet was an open area, and the bathroom was the only separate room. Since the curtains went ceiling to six inches above floor, her feet would be visible if she just ducked behind the curtain. Then she noticed that the curtains covered a two foot area between the window and the edge of the air conditioner/heater unit. She climbed up on it and flattened herself against the wall, Chaplinesque.

The lights came on and she could hear the Suit

walking about, opening and shutting the dresser drawers. Plastic rustled. He was removing the pin-striped suit and yellow silk tie from the plastic bag.

"God, I love this tie," he said. It was all Madeleine could do not to bust out laughing. The next thing out of his mouth brought her back to attention.

"I didn't leave that thing on. I know I didn't. Somebody's been into my computer!" He lifted the lid. She heard him type several keystrokes and shut the lid again.

Footsteps hurried across the room, a door opened and shut, and seconds later she heard him enter Room 203. The laundress hustled down from her perch, dashed out the door and down the hall, ducking into the stairwell just as the door to Room 203 opened.

"I don't care what it means. Just put the damn suit on and let's go!" shouted the older Suit and slammed the door.

CHAPTER 24

The usher took Madeleine's ticket and seated her just before the lights came up on the performance. There was neither time to peruse the program for the costumer credits, nor time to reflect on her recklessness at the DoubleTree. She brought her foot across her knee and held onto it to stop the tapping. Tom Hulce took the stage and she was drawn into to the courtroom drama of *A Few Good Men.*

Between acts several late-comers came slinking to their seats; one such dropped onto the seat next to Madeleine. To be polite, she looked away. When a whiff of Irish Spring rose in the air, the laundress turned to find Cody, in jeans and a pale blue Oxford, beside her. He took her hand and rubbed the palm with his thumb.

"What are you doing here? Why aren't you sleeping?" she whispered.

"Sh-h-h," he whispered back. "Tell you later. Watch."

During the intermission Madeleine filled Cody in on her aborted mission.

"Lucky thing for you, that ledge. It's kinda hard to hide a full figure lady in a hotel room these days. What did you do with the key?" he asked.

"Key?" she echoed. She reached in her right pants pocket and pulled out the key to Room 205. "I guess I forgot to take it back."

"That's okay," said Cody. "I know what to do with it."

The lights blinked, signaling the end of intermission. Cody picked up the programs that marked their spots and stuffed them in his back pocket as he herded Madeleine into her seat.

"May I have my program back please?" Madeleine asked. "I haven't looked at it yet."

"The play's startin' up," he replied. "Do it later."

On stage Lt. Col. Nathan R. Jessup was called to testify. In the audience Madeleine's mind began to wander. She couldn't shut out the thoughts about being in the younger Suit's room. It was sheer providence that the air conditioning unit had been blowing air the full time she was standing on it, otherwise her form would have been clearly visible. But now the Suits knew she was on the hunt. What would they do next?

And then there was the matter of what the Suits were really up to. She and Cody hadn't gotten far enough with surveillance to figure it out. It was definitely big though. She conjured images of bombs and wartime devastation.

"Your Honor!" the prosecutor shouted and Madeleine jerked in her seat.

"Is the color of the Colonel's underwear now a matter of national security?" responded counsel for the defense.

Madeleine turned to Cody in disbelief. He pulled the program out of his pocket and laid it in her lap. There it was in black and white. *A Few Good Men,* written by Aaron Sorkin. Also credited were Scardino, and numerous other of her recent drop-off customers. The bottom dropped out of her stomach.

"You knew?" she mouthed to the carrier.

"Sh-h-h. Watch the play. Talk later," he whispered into her ear. Cody slipped the program back into his pocket and took her hand.

Her face burned and she was glad for the darkness. She stared at the floor in shame and wondered how she could ever have thought that something so mundane could be related to espionage. Cody was right. She always got the cart before the horse. A single tear rolled down her cheek and landed on his arm. Cody gave her hand a quick squeeze and she forced her attention back to the drama.

Twenty minutes later the last round of applause died away. Madeleine turned toward the center aisle to leave, but Cody blocked her path.

"Come on," he said. "We got some cleanin' up to do." He herded her in the opposite direction, down the left aisle and toward the stage.

"Wait! What are we doing?" asked the laundress. She had a bad feeling in the pit of her stomach and her mouth was going dry.

"We made a mess and now we gotta clean it up," answered the carrier. He took her hand and pushed open the door to the hallway. A procession of people moved toward the backstage area, eager to pay their respects to the cast and crew. Madeleine was filled with dread. Ahead she could see the younger Suit's head bobbing as he accepted praise. She looked around frantically for an exit, and Cody tightened his grip on her hand.

"Don't even think about it," he warned. "The Suit deserves to know who got into his computer and why."

"Why does he have to know? Why can't we just leave well enough alone and let him think it was the maid?" Madeleine pleaded. "There's no harm done. I didn't steal anything. Hell, I didn't even see anything!"

A door to the left of them opened and a group of people spilled into the hallway. At the center of the group was the costumer with the flaming red hair. He saw Madeleine and waved his hand.

"You came!" He waded through the crowd toward her. "I was afraid you wouldn't, and I'm so glad you did! What did you think?

"And how wonderful, you brought someone with you!" he said. He turned to Cody and extended a hand. "David Woolard, how do you do?"

Cody shook hands with the costumer, but never released his left hand grip on Madeleine. There was no escape.

"This is my friend Cody." Said Madeleine. "We deliver newspapers together."

"Yeah, Mad's been tellin' me all about you guys. Must be six or eight of you what do your laundry at her place. I know she's gonna miss you. Well, looks like we're up next. Nice meetin' you."

Madeleine thanked the costumer over her shoulder as Cody pulled her to the front of the line and put his arm around her shoulders. The younger Suit ran his hand through straight light-brown hair and adjusted his glasses. He smiled a wide grin and reached out his hand.

"That was a near miss with the suit," he said.

You have no idea, thought the laundress. She shook his hand.

"Thank you so much for bringing it to the hotel. I'll come by and settle up with you tomorrow. Will you be open?"

"Oh, yeah, she'll be there," Cody said. He squeezed Madeleine's shoulder.

"Mr. Sorkin," she started.

"Please, call me Aaron." He laughed and said, "After all, you've seen my dirty laundry."

"Aaron!! We need you!" called out a voice at the end of the hall.

"I'm sorry. I do have to go. See you in the morning?" he said, not waiting for a reply. His spatulate fingertips, nails chewed to the quick, slid up the yellow silk tie and guided the knot back into position below his Adam's apple.

She watched the pin-striped suit disappear into the crowd and contemplated her good fortune. Her toe tapped a happy jig and the heaviness between her shoulders seemed to lift.

"Off the hook—for now," said Cody. He looked at his watch. "Ten-thirty. We still got time for some shut-eye. Let's go."

"How did you get here?" asked Madeleine, threading her way through the throng of people.

"I got a lift with Potter," replied the carrier. "Betty's still in the shop."

"The stake-out come bangin' on the door . . .

something about a blue suit at the 'mat. Seemed like I oughtta check it out. I told 'em I had a key."

"You told them what?!" Madeleine stopped dead in her tracks and twisted to face him.

"Don't get pissed. I don't got a key. The back door was unlocked. It's always unlocked after Rita works, remember? An' I think she comes in sometimes after hours. You oughtta get a security cam. I could do it for you." Cody moved past her, taking her hand. She reeled around, slick leather soles on tile, but caught her balance on the next step.

"Anyway, there was the note on the counter an' no suit, so I knew where you went. No reason to go there. The stake-out told me it was for some big-wig Broadway play guy. I weren't gonna sleep anyway, so I went back home an dressed up."

"Did you tell Potter about the Suits?" Madeleine asked.

"Hell, no," he said. "It'd be one more story in his repertoire. I just hitched a ride to the University. He thinks I was cruisin' for a date."

"He doesn't think there's something going on between you and me?" Madeleine felt deflated.

"Doll," he squeezed her hand, "you're my best kept secret."

"Keep holding hands in public and I won't be."

"Good point," The carrier released his grip. He opened a side exit door and they headed for the parking lot.

CHAPTER 25

At seven-thirty Sunday morning Madeleine arrived at the laundromat to find five bags in a heap at the front door. By eight the laundromat was devoid of customers and the only sound came from seven washers of drop-off.

This was the tail end of the *A Few Good Men* construction crew's laundry; they were still dismantling the set and preparing to go to the Kennedy Center for the next leg of their journey. The laundress stapled the note they left to a ticket and tagged each of the washers. It was satisfying to know the role each of them played in the production. She could now picture them at work on a set she had seen.

Madeleine had a pot of coffee brewing on the counter in the lounge area when Cody came in from his route. She poured him a cup and pushed the cream and sugar toward him. He pulled up a chair, turned it backwards and sat down.

"That stuff's for sissies," he said. "I like mine black as sin." He made a face and kicked his leg out. "Damn, that's strong enough to suck chrome off a bumper!"

"Too strong for you, sissy?" she asked with a smile. She poured herself a cup, added two spoons of sugar and filled it to the brim with cream. Steam rose from the cup and miniscule oil beads rolled around the surface of the dark golden liquid. "You can always doctor strong coffee, but there isn't anything that makes weak coffee better . . . kinda like men, don't you think?"

"I think you hung around Jerry too long an' it made you bitter." He changed the subject.

"So what's the deal with Rita? She workin' second or you doin' a double? Don't that get old, always havin' to be here?"

"It's not any different from you being on the route seven days a week."

"Touché. First time in—"

101

"Four years. Yes, I remember. You'd think Betty was your girlfriend, the way you talk about her. Did you ever actually *have* a girlfriend? You never talk about anyone." The laundress cocked her head as a washer broke into its spin cycle. She twirled the spoon in her coffee and licked the scum off the back of it.

"I don't 'kiss and tell,'" said Cody. "I didn't notice you bein' dissatisfied last night. You got a problem?"

Madeleine looked into his azure eyes. They were red-rimmed and fine lines ran from the corners toward the temples. There was nothing to indicate deception, but something was off. She could feel it. Her foot could feel it and was starting to tap.

"Yeah, I got a problem," she echoed. "My house is torn up and my boyfriend for the last eight years died chasing a burglar in our house. I've been assaulted, interrogated, humiliated, and then I slept with someone I know nothing about.

"Do you realize that? I don't know the first thing about you. I don't know where you live, who you hang out with, what you do for fun, what kind of relationships you've had—nothing. All I know is that you drive a Toyota named Betty, run a newspaper route and are friendly with the Pakki who runs the IHOP."

"Don't call him a 'Pakki'."

"There aren't even any family pictures in the house," she plowed on. And then there's that thing about your mother. I don't know what that's about."

"You don't forget nothin,' do ya." It wasn't a question. He squared his shoulders and let out a breath. "Okay. That's fair. I don't talk about my business cuz it's nobody else's business. In my family we're like that. And no, we're not Mafia.

"Mom died when the house burned down in New Jersey. I was twelve and I couldn't get her out."

"Oh my God!" Madeleine was mortified. "What about your dad? Was he there?"

"Nah. Away on business. She was in the morgue three days before he got the news."

"That must have been awful," said Madeleine. "Now I feel like a shit for saying all that."

"It was a long time ago and I learned early to keep my trap shut. Dad was OSS way back. You know, 'loose lips sink ships.'

"Anyway, we moved a few times. I lived with other relatives for a while and then came down here to visit. I liked it, so I stayed. End o' story." He drained the cup and set it on the counter.

"Not quite," said the laundress. She poured another cup of coffee, doctored it, and pushed the spoon through the liquid once. "So, what's your last name?"

"Cody," he replied.

"Your last name is Cody? People always call you by your last name?"

"When you got a name like mine, it's better that way." He pulled off his hat and ran a hand through flattened hair. It sprang back to life, a few silver strands glistening in the morning sunlight. He replaced the hat, brim turned backward.

"And that name is . . ." said Madeleine, tapping the spoon on the cup.

"William Joseph Donovan Cody."

"'Wild Bill,'" said Madeleine. "I'm impressed. Did you know him?"

"Nah," Cody replied. "He died when I was three."

"So your father knew him," she fished.

"Hard not to. The intelligence community was pretty small, and Donovan made it his business to know everybody. It was sort of a trademark, and real smart too. Folks'll do just about anything you ask, if you treat 'em right.

"In combat he walked the lines at Landres-St George to encourage his troops in a no-win situation. He showed 'em he wasn't afraid to stick his own neck out, and he wasn't asking them to do anything he wouldn't do himself.

"Lotsa people think his first intel gig was OSS, but he was in it way before that. Office of Coordination of Information, COI for short, was the first agency, then OSS and then CIA. He ran 'em all *and* he's the most decorated man in US history. He's the only one to get all four of the top medals: Medal of Honor, Distinguished Service Cross, Distinguished Service Medal, and the National Security Medal.

"That last cup spoken for?" he asked as he drained the pot into his cup.

A warm shaft of light filtered through the room from the window overlooking the parking lot. The laundress eased her stool around to the other side of the counter so she could warm her back in the sun and sit closer to Cody. As she moved in beside him, the hair on Madeleine's left arm stood on end and heat traveled through her body. Their eyes met.

"'Danger danger, Will Robinson,'" he said softly. "You're gonna blow my cover." He twirled his chair so that it faced the door, sat down and tipped back onto two legs. He scanned the lot and Madeleine turned around to see what he was watching.

A navy blue Crown Victoria pulled up to the front of the building and the younger Suit stepped out. He was dressed in layers for the changing fall weather, a pale yellow sweater draped and tied fashionably around blue Polo-clad shoulders. As he entered the laundromat, he pulled a wallet from the side pocket of his khaki pants.

The laundress sucked in air and straightened her back as she rose from the stool. The moment of truth had come.

"Good morning, Aaron," she said, crossing to the drop-off counter. She gave him her most generous smile. "I guess we've got some settling-up to do. You can put your wallet away. This one's on the house."

The playwright looked surprised but happy. "You liked the play? It's going to be a movie. I'm already writing the screenplay."

Out of the corner of her eye she saw Cody grin. She was on trial.

"Your play was a real eye-opener. I mean, I didn't know you wrote plays. I thought you were in a different line of work." She looked away.

"What sort of work?" he asked. He dropped the wallet back into his pocket.

"Um, national security . . . not necessarily ours." Her foot twitched and her toes retracted in the sneakers. She tried to meet his gaze.

"You mean you thought I was, we were spies? How did you . . . ?" A vertical dent formed beside each bushy eyebrow.

"I don't know," she said in desperation. "It was all those different kinds of clothes. You could have been anything or everything. That's what made me start wondering."

"It was the line about the Colonel's underwear that really nailed it," said Cody from across the room.

"But how did you know about the line if you hadn't seen the play?" The bushy brows came together, the dents forming a perfect M. His head turned sideways and he looked away.

"Wait a minute. You were the one who got into my laptop."

"Uh huh," she said. She put her foot back so that the red rubber toe rested vertical to the floor and couldn't tap.

Cody got up and strolled over to the counter. "In her defense, she didn't see nothing last night. You came home too fast. She saw what you was workin' on last week while we was bagging papers behind the IHOP."

"What? You broke into my room while you doing what?" He looked from Madeleine's face to Cody's in confusion.

"No, we didn't break into your room. We watched you from the car while you were working on the computer," said Madeleine. This was not going well. She shot a pleading look at Cody.

"We deliver newspapers and we were bagging papers in the car," supplied the carrier.

"She was worried about you two and what you were up to. I just gave her a crash course in stake-out to show her you can't tell everything from somebody's boxers. I gave Mad the binoculars. I didn't tell her to go through your hotel room. She pulled that one on her own." He dug into the watch pocket of his Levis and produced the hotel key. "I think this is yours."

"I really thought you were into something weird and this town has a lot going on," said Madeleine. "There's FBI downtown, the CIA place down the road here on Emmett and some big underground thingy in Culpeper. You could have been planning some kind of terrorist attack."

Madeleine's voice rose as she built her defense. Cody gave a warning look and she dropped her pitch. "I guess I shouldn't have said all that, should I. Well, what would *you* do in my place?"

"I see your point," said the playwright. "I will never work on anything else where anyone can watch me again. I don't think I'll even collaborate with anyone else. God, this makes me paranoid. I could press charges, but under the circumstances, I won't. This just stays between the three of us."

"Agreed," said Cody.

"You bet," said Madeleine, thanking her lucky stars.

"So Aaron," she said with a wink, "Would you

please autograph my program?"

"I guess so," he said with a shrug. The laundress hustled out to the Datsun to get her playbill before he could change his mind. Sorkin turned to Cody and said, "One of our crew told me that her partner died last week when a burglar broke into her house. Is that true?"

"Yeah," said Cody. "She was runnin' my route while I was at the paper. She thought you and your buddy paid someone to do a hit 'cuz she was on to you. Didn't help none that the same guy got in my car while she was in the IHOP droppin' a bundle."

"What happened?" asked the playwright. He glanced out the glass toward the parking lot; Madeleine was still pawing through the debris in her back seat.

"Nailed him with the scissors, right in the leg. Whoever he is, he's one sore motherfucker now."

"Damn!" said Aaron. He felt new appreciation for the laundress. "He's probably one pissed motherfucker too. I hope you're keeping an eye on her. He might come back. Is she getting any police protection?"

"Nah. The police think it's domestic. If they're watchin', it's to catch her up, not to help."

"Well, good luck with that," said the playwright. "You know, this could make a hell of a story."

"An' you don't know the half of it," said Cody with a laugh.

CHAPTER 26

"But you don't understand, Detective; we can't plan a funeral with no body! You told me he died of a broken neck. How could it possibly take this long to run an autopsy?"

Madeleine propped the phone in the crook of her neck and rolled a cart over to the third washer. She opened the lid and unloaded the contents of the washer.

"What am I supposed to tell his family?" she asked. She tossed the clothes into an open dryer and secured the ticket to the door with a magnet. "They're not the kind of people who have a quiet memorial service six months from now. They're the kind that have an open-casket wake. His brothers would have him sitting up in the box with a beer in his hand if they could. Yeah . . . all right. I'll tell them. What else can I do? Goodbye."

She punched the phone off and set it on the counter. Lifting the lid on an ornamental metal box next to the register, she grabbed a handful of quarters. She inserted three into the dryer and hit the start button.

In the lounge Cody was chatting with the woman who came in the green Ford. She had arrived and filled a jumbo washer while Sorkin was autographing Madeleine's play bill. As the jumbo entered its final spin, she said something to the carrier and ducked out of the laundromat.

Madeleine finished moving the drop-off and joined Cody in the lounge. The sunny room was approaching seventy-five degrees, warm enough to be uncomfortable in a long-sleeved shirt but not enough to turn on the AC. The laundress propped open the door as the carrier rolled up the sleeves on his Oxford shirt to just below the elbow.

"Cozying up to your next victim?" She rested her bulk on the stool and fanned herself with a magazine.

"That woman has become one of my best regulars, but she is one weird bird. How'd you get her to talk to you? She won't say boo to me," said the laundress, eyeing the newsprint smears on Cody's shirt. She imagined peeling the shirt from his back and running her fingers over his torso.

"Stop it," said the carrier. He adjusted his watch.

"Stop what?" asked Madeleine, all innocence.

"Don't quibble. You know what I mean. We got trouble enough.

"That regular o' yours is Ellen. You know, B an' E, Bob an' Ellen? Anyway, she's been runnin' their route cuz Bob's out sick. I offered to take some of the route, the bundle drops, so she don't have to get out the vehicle. I told her about the guy gettin' into Betty. She said she heard about it and she'd take me up on the offer."

"Mighty magnanimous after that business with the Orchard subdivision," observed Madeleine.

"That weren't Ellen's doin. She's just married to the jerk, like you an' Jerry."

"Spare me," said the laundress. "We were not married.

"Do you think we'll ever have a real life? I still see that white car everywhere I go and Detective Knight isn't releasing Jerry's body, so I'm still stuck in that mess. At this rate I'll be stuck with Jerry's family forever. They keep bugging me about the funeral plans. Maybe I'll sick Janey on the detective. She probably could get blood out of a turnip."

"I gotta give it to ya, Mad. You're creative. I saw Janey ream the circ man once cuz her carrier couldn't get the toss up to the front door. She expected him to hike it over a ten-foot security fence. Then there was some business about waking her Doberman. I think the circ man hadda get him a whole new heini when she was done."

The carrier paced in front of the window, checking each of the hanging flower baskets. He brushed the potting soil from his fingers over the trash can in the corner.

"Dry as a bone. Where's the watering can?"

Madeleine pointed over her shoulder and Cody disappeared into the back room. It was nice to have someone helpful in her life for a change. It seemed that everyone else either abdicated responsibility entirely or they wanted her to pay a guilt tax. One didn't have to accept guilt but it was still a lot of energy wasted in combat.

"A frikkin' bunch of Eyores," she muttered.

"What's that?" asked Cody behind her.

Madeleine jumped. "I should be used to it by now," she said, "but you still scare the bejezus out of me. I never hear you coming."

He stared up at the hanging baskets. "Guess I'll have to work on that.

"What's an Eyore?"

"You know. Winnie the Pooh. The terminally morose donkey. I was just thinking how my life has been full of them until now. You're different."

"Not an Eeyore?"

"Definitely not," replied Madeleine.

He poured the last of the water into the basket by the door and set the can down. A drip formed on the edge of the basket and a stream of brownish water dribbled onto the floor. The carrier moved the can with his foot so that it caught most of the liquid, but the floor was already spattered.

"I got it," said Cody as Madeleine started up from her perch to find a rag.

"See, that's what I mean," she said. "You don't wait until I've gotten up and wiped it before you say you'll get it. You actually act like you give a damn."

"Well, don't broadcast it. I got a reputation to uphold." Cody returned the rag and checked the back door. It was unlocked. He slid the bolt back in place and joined Madeleine who was now folding laundry at the front counter.

"Rita just stands there like a bump on a log and

never takes initiative," Madeleine continued. "The exception is when she wants something, and then she's superhuman. Oh, and you get to pay extra for it too. 'Look what I did for you,' as if you are utterly worthless or incompetent and couldn't live without her.

"And how is it that she who does so little stays skinny while I do most of the cleaning around here and I stay fat?" She waved a pair of black socks at him.

"You're not fat, doll. I've seen fat and you're not it. You're five-nine and you got the weight to support it." The carrier smiled and dropped his voice. "I don't like 'em skinny. You know what the deal is with Rita? Crystal."

"Crystal? Who's she?" Madeleine bagged up the order, weighed and tagged it. Then she pulled over the next cart loaded with warm dry clothes.

"Crystal ain't a she. It's a drug. Meth, speed, crystal, whatever ya wanna call it. It's trouble." The carrier pulled out the socks and matched the pairs.

"How can you tell?" asked Madeleine.

"Look at her teeth. Look at how she gets erratic, when she goes off on ya. Look at her borrowin' habit." Cody straightened his stack of socks and fished out the underwear from the cart.

"Maybe I'm wrong and she's one of them manics. They look the same in a meltdown," he continued his line of thought. "Either way, you got trouble. Manics like to spend money when they're up—money they don't got. A lot of 'em don't like the drugs the shrinks give for it, so they do their own drugs—alcohol or pot. I'm not knockin' the manics; lotsa great people are that way, and they're the life o' the party when they're up. But it's a bad mix in some people."

"Hmm. If it's speed, do you think she's selling it here? What do I do?" asked the laundress. She took a T-shirt from the cart, turned it upside down and shook it twice; then she snapped it flat on the counter, front side down, and folded it in thirds. When she was done the shirt was a perfect rectangle, the size of a piece of typing paper.

Cody pushed the underwear and sock piles to the end of the counter and followed Madeleine's example with the T-shirts. "Ya set her up and let the detective take her down." The carrier grinned with satisfaction. "He wants to solve a crime. Let's help him do his job."

CHAPTER 27

Madeleine wasn't so sure about the first leg of Cody's plan. It involved hiring a new attendant at the laundromat. Cody had caught Winnie, the "Church Lady" carrier, just when the ten o'clock service let out at Free Will Christian Church. She hadn't yet gone to bed. Was she interested in a temporary assignment in return for some of her route? Yes indeedy; she'd be right over.

"So how long do I have to keep her and how much are we going to tell her?" asked Madeleine, feeling her grip on her establishment erode.

"As long as it takes and as little as possible," answered the carrier. "Winnie likes to talk, so we might feed her some disinformation."

"What kind of disinformation?"

"Where you're stayin,' why you need another person workin' here, what's goin' on with Rita. She definitely don't need to know we're settin' Rita up. We need to think of her like a funnel."

"A funnel?"

"Yeah, for information. We tell her something we want Rita to know but can't tell directly."

"You mean we're lying to the Church Lady?"

"I prefer to call it 'selective inference,'" said the carrier. "It's not big whoppers. It's just not the whole truth. It's true you need a break. You been workin' your ass off for years. No vacations, no fun. Jerry just died and you got the perfect excuse. Your customers get somebody new to talk to and the place'll be clean. Winnie knows how to do clean. All you have to do is teach her the drawer stuff and how to fold clothes the way you do. I think a week is all we need."

Madeleine organized all the drop-offs for the *A Few*

Good Men crew so that they were in front on the shelf. The rest she knew would come later in the day. She pulled out the paper bag with the bong and set it next to the laundry she'd done the previous day. She touched her head.

"Still lumpy?" asked Cody.

"Uh huh," she replied. "Feels like a lifetime ago. It's not too bad though. Your method works pretty well. Maybe we should try it again later."

"Copy that," said Cody and headed out the door. "I'll be back."

The after-church crowd began to descend and Madeleine had no more time to think about 'the Master Plan," as she envisioned it. She traded quarter rolls for tens and handed a cups of crayons and blank paper to several small children whose mothers were negligent and/or deaf. Those same mothers were ignorant in the art of cleaning up after themselves, so the laundress donned an apron and chased their soap from the rims with hot water. With a rag she absorbed the excess and wiped down the tops of the machines.

Soon the machines were tidy, the floor swept, and the trash bins emptied. Listening to the machines changing from rinse into spin cycles, Madeleine felt idle and empty. She went into the back room, restocked the soap and piled the empty cardboard boxes by the back door. The sensation in her stomach was a churning that seemed to spread out to her fingertips. It was accompanied by a restlessness that activity did not dispel.

The laundress sat on the tile floor before the soap closet, pulled her knees to her chest and sobbed. Years of living by trial and error with Jerry were over, and with them went the knowledge of how every day would end. She wept for all the promises made and broken, for the waste of both their lives. Then she wept for the uncertain terrain of new love.

"Oh honey, I'm so sorry. I came as quick as I could. He didn't tell me it was this bad," said a soft woman's voice from the doorway to the front.

Madeleine looked up, tears blurring her vision. The apparition was silhouetted in the doorway and it took Madeleine a second to realize that this was in fact the Church Lady. The laundress grasped the steel door knob and pulled herself to her feet. She dried her eyes on the apron and wiped her hands down her pants.

"I'm Madeleine. I'm sorry I'm such a mess. I'm just having a bad moment. Come into the lounge and I'll fix some coffee."

"I never touch the stuff, but if that pot will boil water, I've got some tea in my bag." She rooted through her purse and produced a tea bag.

The two women sat in the lounge sipping coffee and tea, talking about the job description and learning about each other. Across the room children argued over who got the cornflower blue "crown" and who got the pink. A couple of college students were parked in front of the wide screen TV, one cheering, one booing the referee's call in a football game.

Winnie was not at all what Madeleine had expected. She had pictured the pastor's wife as older, matronly and built like an apple dumpling with silver hair. Winnie turned out to be thirty-something, trim and dark haired. She was still dressed for Sunday services, in a calf-length navy polyester dress with small white polka dots.

"When will you have time to sleep?" asked Madeleine. "I'm beginning to think Cody never sleeps. Every time I think he's at his dad's house sleeping, he shows up here and then leaves, saying he has something to do. He never says he's going home to sleep."

"That's because he's in love with you," said Winnie. "He can't sleep."

"Do what?" said Madeleine. Her face flushed hot.

"Has been since the first day he laid eyes on you. Didn't you know that? You're all he talks about," said the pastor's wife.

"He doesn't talk much. Doesn't seem to believe in it," commented Madeleine. She frowned.

"Cody doesn't have to say much. You forget; I see him almost every morning when I take the returns back to the paper. I'm never on the dock when they load up, but I drop the returns on my way home." She pressed the tea bag against the back of the spoon, wrapped the string around it and wrung it out over her cup.

"It doesn't take a rocket scientist to figure out that you're the same 'friend' he has who's 'hooked on a drunk and headed for trouble.' He asked me once if any of the drunks I see at the Mission ever get sober. I said 'no, not without Jesus.' 'Well, that'll never happen,' he said.

"Now he calls me up and tells me his new recruit needs help at her day job. I already know what happened at the IHOP, and I know that the man who died during the B&E lived with the woman who was Cody's new recruit. That woman is you. QED." She sat back in her chair and waited for Madeleine to take it all in.

Madeleine let out a breath. "All those things are true, but it doesn't mean he's in love with me."

"Look," said Winnie. She leaned forward and rested her forearms on the counter. "Consider that the rest of our conversations consist of Cosmo, his dad being out of town, and will the Red Sox ever win the pennant. Now do you see what I mean? The real question isn't about Cody. The real question is about you. Do you love him?"

Under the counter Madeleine's red rubber toe was tapping a furious beat. There was no easy abort switch for this conversation. How had she let it get so far?

"Winnie, I don't think we should be talking about Cody. I don't think he'd appreciate us discussing his business in public."

The pastor's wife eyed Madeleine for a moment. "That may be true, but he is my friend and has been for ten years or more. If I am going to help the woman he has lost his heart to, I want to know where she stands."

Madeleine's eye's welled up. She wiped them away with the back of her hand and looked away.

"I don't know what you want me to say. I don't know if I'm in love with him or if it's just rebound. I thought I was in love with Jerry. I don't know when it stopped being love and when it started being habit. You're in the sin business, which one is the sin: staying with someone you don't love anymore or leaving them for someone else? I was going to split up with Jerry but he died before I could tell him. He always said I was going to leave him."

The dam broke and tears rushed down her face. The Church Lady rose and looked behind the counter. She handed Madeleine some paper towels and patted her hand.

"He did his best to push you away. It was a self-fulfilling prophecy. You mustn't let guilt run your life like that. Guilt is a habit too, the worst. If you want this to work with Cody, you have to put that behind you. Jesus didn't tell the adulteress to go burn in Hell. He said "Go and sin no more." That's John 8:11. Look it up sometime.

"Why don't you go freshen up in the bathroom? I'll watch the front. When you come back, you can give me the cook's tour." Winnie glanced around the laundromat and smiled. "I think I'm going to do fine here."

CHAPTER 28

Cody returned at five o'clock, showered, shaved and clothed in a red plaid button-up and boot cut Levis. The well-oiled tips of a pair of Red Wings peeked out from under his jeans. He scanned the laundromat.

"Did Winnie come?" He leaned back against the counter, removed his navy blue baseball hat and inspected the bill.

"Of course she came," said Madeleine. "She came in her Sunday-go-to-meeting clothes. We talked a while and I showed her around and gave her a key."

"When does she start?" He scratched at the Red Sox emblem with his nail and brushed off the offending speck.

"Tomorrow."

"Tomorrow? Really?" Cody was impressed. "You sure didn't waste no time."

"I like her," Madeleine confessed. "I expected some old lady evangelist, but she's not like that at all. She talked out of the Bible, but she didn't preach. Her brand of religion isn't too bad. She's all about people. I think I could get used to having her here. You know, if Rita gets busted, I'll have to find someone else."

"Yeah, I thought about that," said the carrier. "Well, strike while the iron is hot."

"Speaking of which, those two women watching the movie have dryers about to stop. I'm all cleancd up and the drawer's done. We could leave when they're finished." She rocked her head back and forth to some inner music.

"Great minds," said Cody, donning his hat. "Ya hungry?"

121

"Uh huh." Madeleine straightened the bags of laundry on the shelf. She stared at one bag and then turned it sideways. "Darn it. She did it again."

"Did what?"

"Mixed the bags up."

"Winnie?"

"No. Rita. Two of the *A Few Good Men* cast have names that sound alike: Malina and Molina," the laundress explained. "She got them mixed up before and it was a mess. I told her to have them spell the names out or write them on the tickets themselves. Good thing they both have the minimum eight dollar order and they don't wear the same kinds of clothes." She turned the bag back so that the tag showed. "It looks like a straight switch and I can just move the tags. I don't want to have to call them and I don't want Winnie to have to deal with unhappy customers on her first day. This brings me to something you and I haven't talked about."

"What's that?" asked the carrier.

"I don't have a phone number where they can call me if there's a meltdown, like a flood or a customer hissy."

"We'll have to do a radio relay. Nobody gets dad's number."

"What's a radio relay?"

"Winnie calls the paper. Circ man gets on the radio and calls me. When he gets me he patches the call directly into the radio. We have special channels just for that. Lotsa carriers use CB, ham radios or Walkie-Talkies. I use a Walkie-Talkie, and I have a mobile unit I can rig up. It's handy when Betty's sick. I don't want her to ruin my record."

"Rub it in, rub it in," said Madeleine. "Guess you don't have to worry about that anymore. I already ruined it."

"That don't count. We showed up to do the route and we wouldda finished it if that asshole hadn't got in the car an' assaulted you. The papers were all bagged, an' all Potter hadda do was toss 'em and fill tubes.

"Hello, Earth to Mad. Are you listenin' to me?" asked the carrier. He waved a hand in front of her face. Madeleine stared right through him and then snapped to attention.

"What?" she asked. "I'm sorry. I was thinking nice smutty thoughts. You were saying something about showing up to do the route?"

"Never mind," Cody replied. "It don't matter anyway. Smut's good. Keep it up. It'll come in handy later." He lowered his volume.

"Looks like those dryers stopped. I'm gonna set up for the Rita gig while they fold their stuff. Let me know when they're done."

"I want to watch," said Madeleine. She followed the carrier into the back room. He stopped abruptly and swung around. Madeleine slammed into his chest.

"Ow!" She stepped back and winced, pulling her arms in to massage her mashed bosom.

"No," said Cody. "No watching. You'll give it away. I shouldda waited 'til you were gone. You wanna do something? Get my tool box outa the Datsun."

His tone of voice left no room for argument. The laundress left the room and returned a few minutes later, lugging the heavy gray metal toolbox. She shoved the mop bucket aside with her foot and set the box on the floor by the utility sink.

"What do you men carry in these things? Uranium?" asked Madeleine. She rotated her arm over her shoulder to release a kink, then shook the arm out.

"Guys got tool boxes; women got handbags. Same difference. Now scat!" he shooed her away.

CHAPTER 29

"Is he still back there?" Madeleine asked Cody as she turned from Greenbrier onto Hydraulic Road. In the rear view mirror a white car also turned onto Hydraulic from the same direction.

"Yeah. Don't act like you're lookin.' I want him to think we forgot about him. Let's get some burgers at Hardees and swap seats. I'm ready to ditch this guy."

The white sedan was parked on the exit side of the Hardees lot as the pair emerged with their bags and drinks. Cody started the Datsun and darted out the entrance onto Rio Road just as the traffic light gave the left turn signal. At Earlysville Road he took a right and headed north past the reservoir into rural Albemarle County.

"I think we lost him," said the carrier, looking in the rear view mirror. He dug into his French fries and popped a few in his mouth. The road was winding and some of the bends sharp, but not a fry dropped on his lap.

Madeleine was not so lucky. Her white shirt was soon spattered with Coke and ketchup. She licked the salt off her fingers and wiped a smear of ketchup off the seat between her legs. The sight of the smear brought a flood of memories of the assault in Betty, and with them, all the old anxieties.

"Where are we going? It's going to be dark soon. Are we going to be back in time to run the route?"

"One at a time, doll," said Cody. "We have a place in Greene County, so it's not far. What's the problem? Why are you diggin' in the seat, Mad?"

Cody pulled the car over, shut off the engine and pulled up the brake. He took Madeleine's left hand and lifted it to see what she was scrubbing. In the waning light the smear was barely visible now but the seat had acquired a patch of tiny white lint balls from the napkins. The laundress slumped against the window and stared at the fence line. He let the brake down and pulled her toward him.

"It ain't always gonna be like this. Someday you'll look at whatcha spilled, and it'll just be ketchup. Just takes time." He stroked her cheek and brushed her hair back behind her ear. "An' maybe a little R&R." He kissed her lips lightly and felt her energy shift. "Definitely some R&R. That's my security on it; the rest comes later."

Twenty minutes later the carrier turned off the main road and headed down a gravel road past a line of mail boxes opposite a long-abandoned country store. The road paralleled a creek and then veered sharply and began a steep ascent. A rusty sign announced the end of state maintenance.

"'All hope abandon, ye who enter here.'" quoted the laundress as they passed the sign. "Is this Shifflett Hollow?" She imagined an unpainted house with an outhouse and a still set up in the woods behind it. There were stories, spanning both sides of the Blue Ridge, about the Shiffletts and Morrises, two families that wed and scrapped with each other like Hatfields and McCoys.

"Nah," replied Cody. "This is Dogwood Valley. There are Shiffletts up here, but mostly it's hunting cabins and folks from northern Virginia or Maryland—retired government people who just wanna be left the hell alone. It's still cheap to live up here and it's quiet. The most noise you're gonna hear is a chain saw or someone doin' target practice."

The road twisted to the left and the tires spun on gravel. Cody found a bare patch of rock where the tires got better purchase and made the bend safely.

"Four wheel drive is whatcha need here. It keeps away the average folks."

"That's me: Jane Q. Average," said Madeleine, falling back into her doldrums.

Cody pulled the car into a driveway and up to a heavy steel cattle gate. He engaged the emergency brake but left the engine running. He faced the laundress.

"Doll, you are anything but. How many people get out of the situation you were in Friday night? For all you knew, that guy was gonna do you, kill you and then dump your body somewhere. Not only did you get out of it, you hurt him and sent him runnin' home to his mamma. You got cajones and that is not average. And stop dumpin' on yourself cuz Jerry died. That weren't your doin.' He couldda tripped on the stairs and broke his neck gettin' up for a beer. Oh yeah, and one more thing—"

"There's more?" Madeleine groaned. She now knew how it felt to be on the wrong end of Columbo's cigar.

"So what if ya read the signs wrong on the Suits. Even I thought there was something funny goin' on. But there's no harm done, and nobody caught you hiding behind the curtain. I egged you on, so I'm as responsible as you—maybe more, since I had other reasons for wantin' to run surveillance. I'm not sorry I did that. Now I know what kinda person you are and how good you do in a pinch. You got one big imagination and an even bigger mouth, but you keep your trap shut when it counts, and that's what matters.

"Enough said. Now you drive and I'll open the gate," said Cody and he hopped out of the car before Madeleine could voice an opinion. She slung her leg over the gear shift and heaved her bulk across the gap. In the headlight he fiddled with something on the back side of the gate post. The carrier swung the gate aside and she navigated through the opening. After securing the gate, he got back in the vehicle, rolled down the window and directed her down a narrow lane for a quarter mile. The lane opened into an area large enough to park four or five cars and was rimmed with azalea bushes. A single story, shingle-shod bungalow bid a warm welcome with a soft light glowing in the right front window.

The laundress shut her eyes and inhaled the pine scent down to her solar plexus. Crickets ticked and chirped, and a twig snapped as some small creature scuttled through the underbrush nearby.

"Come on, doll," said the carrier into her ear. He got out and opened the driver's side door. Madeleine took another breath and savored the scent; then she stepped out onto the gravel driveway. She followed him to the front door and listened to the night sounds from the woods as he fed the key into the lock. Her stomach fluttered and her toe began to tap. She shifted her weight and cleared her throat, to obscure the nervousness. As the door fell open, Cody took her hand and pulled her inside.

Madeleine was surprised at the décor. Far from the hunting cabin she expected, this place was warm and comfortable. The U-shaped kitchen to her right had a refrigerator, stove, dishwasher and microwave oven. A butcher block table stood sentry at the hub of the U, neatly topped with a red checkered cloth place mat, bottle of 1982 Beringer cabernet and two wine glasses.

"Nice place. It doesn't look like a hunter's cabin," Madeleine remarked.

"Gotta check on something," said Cody. He doffed his hat and hung it on a hook on the wall. "Make yourself at home. Bathroom's the first door off the hall. Open that bottle o' wine if you want; cork screw's in the first drawer, left side." He disappeared down the hallway off the far end of the living room to her left.

Madeleine found the cork screw exactly where Cody had indicated. The drawer was filled with kitchen utensils, each placed to maximize the space. She marveled at this. In her own kitchen the drawers were crowded and the only rule for finding an item was the rule of depth: the most recently-used items being close to the top of the pile.

"Ya gonna pop that cork or just stare in the drawer?" asked Cody from the hallway. He finished wiping his hands on a hand towel and turned away without waiting for a reply. A moment later he reappeared.

He flicked a switch on the wall by the doorway and light streamed down from recessed ceiling lights above a built-in bookcase. Soft music of a Latin salsa flowed from a pair of oak Infinity Reference speakers flanking the bookcase.

"A little music, a little vino" said the carrier. He took a glass of wine from Madeleine and held it under her nose. "Shut yer eyes. Now tell me what you smell."

"Raspberries and something tangy," she replied. She opened her eyes and took a sip from her own glass. "It's almost like pepper."

"We might make a wine snob outa you yet," said Cody, pleased with her observations.

"We?" asked Madeleine. "Who is this 'we,' Kimo Sabe?"

"Just an expression," he replied and nodded toward the bottle. "Do ya like it?"

"Umm hmm," said the laundress and swallowed. "Very good." The wine left a warmth all the way to her tummy and the miseries of the day began to fade.

She meandered around the living room as she sipped. It was a comfortable space with a dark blue leather couch and two matching arm chairs facing a moderate sized Jotul wood stove. Through the glass door of the stove a few coals glowed red and Madeleine could feel the heat emanating from them. She looked down at the oval braided rug that ran from the couch to the edge of a black metal pan protruding from under the stove. There was no ash on it, nor any wood chips.

"This is really clean, but don't you worry about a fire? That rug is awfully close to the stove, Cody," she said. She shuddered and wished she hadn't said it.

"Nah," said the carrier. "The rug's fire-retardant, and I always keep it clean. I got a special metal Shop-Vac just for that. I got this down to a science, how to get the most outa the Jotul with the least mess."

Cody crossed the room to a tall brass box situated two feet to the right of the stove. He rested his glass on the bookshelf, lifted the lid and pulled out two twenty-two inch locust logs. With the logs balanced in his right arm, he took a pair of kitchen tongs from the stove caddy, re-arranged the coals and then loaded the wood. The locust snapped and popped as it caught fire behind the glass. The carrier replaced the tongs, tidied up with the brush and pan, then dumped the debris back into the stove.

"Jotul-eh-he-ho!" he lifted his glass and toasted the stove.

"Yodel-eh-he-ho!" Madeleine returned the toast.

The laundress poured herself a little more cabernet and offered some to Cody. She perused the bookshelf and pulled out a tome on the Civil War. She flipped through it and returned it to the shelf. She scanned a few more and turned to Cody.

"For a Yankee, you sure have a lot of books on the Civil War."

"I beg yer pardon. My mother was not a Yankee; she was a Virginian, so that qualifies me as a Virginian. And that was the War of Northern Aggression, if yer gonna be picky." The carrier moved in behind her, took the glass from her hand and set it on the bookshelf. He set his beside it and took her hand.

"Dance with me," he whispered against her cheek and wrapped his arm around her waist.

"I don't dance, not this kind. I don't think—"

"Then don't think. Shh," he cooed. "I'll lead. You follow."

"But—"

"Shh." Cody kissed her and tightened his grip around her waist. His movements were slow and deliberate, hips swaying in perfect eight beat time with the music. Madeleine fell into the side-to-side rolling rhythm of the Machata and relaxed against his body. She rested her head on his shoulder and felt the heat rise through her body when he nibbled her ear and kissed her goose egg.

"Does it hurt now?" he asked.

"Not anymore," she replied and looked his eyes.

"See, I told ya I could make it all better."

He laid her left hand on his shoulder and stroked her chin and down her throat lightly with the back of his index finger. Madeleine inhaled sharply as Cody's hand found its way under her T-shirt, freeing hooks and eyes, and back up across her breast. She reached both hands behind his head and pulled his lips to hers. She teased his upper lip with her tongue and unbuttoned his shirt, pushing it aside so she could feel his bare chest against her breasts. Their tongues mingled as they explored each other.

"That's a mighty hard belt buckle, Cody," said Madeleine, coming up for air.

"That's not my belt buckle, doll."

"I know," she said, smiling. She freed the last two front buttons and the sleeves. The shirt fell to the floor, followed closely by her own shirt and bra.

Cody cupped both of Madeleine's pendulous breasts, trapping the nipples between his thumbs and index fingers. He squeezed gently and moved his lips down her throat to the hollow between her breasts. Her heart pounded and her legs grew weak.

"Couch!" she breathed heavy into his curls. "I can't stand anymore!"

Into the soft leather sofa they tumbled, each racing to pull the other's pants off first. Shoes, boots, socks and underwear flew until there was nothing but skin on skin.

Madeleine reached down and caressed the velvet shaft between them. She ran her fingers from tip to base, encircled him and brought her hand up, gradually increasing pressure. Cody's eyes glazed over; he pulled her down on him and kissed her hard. Rolling toward the edge of the sofa, he locked her in place with his leg, reached into his jeans pocket and pulled out a small foil packet.

"God, I want you without this," he huffed.

"Me too,' she said, repositioning. "Here, let me." Madeleine unrolled the sleeve onto him and coaxed him back up to speed.

Cody combed through her fur and pressed his middle finger against the heart of the nub. Sliding the finger down farther, he slipped between the folds and drew fluid. Pressing his thumb above the nub, his finger stroked across the opening until her body began to quiver. She pulled her leg over his hip and guided him inside, as the heat pulsed through her.

"Cody?" She said when they were both spent.

"Yeah, Mad?" He kissed the top of her head and played with her hair.

"This couch is bigger than my car, but not by much." She propped herself on one elbow. "How about that bigger rink?"

"We got one 'o them and a bathroom too. Want some more wine?"

"Sure. More calories. Drink 'em and burn 'em."

The carrier grinned. "That's the ticket. Let's go!"

The stack of clothes on the stool by the old claw foot tub was as neat and square as Madeleine had ever folded herself. She hooked the bra harness and wondered if

Cody had ever been in the military. Military people could be very obsessed with neatness. Cody had dressed while she was still in the shower, and it irked her that she still hadn't seen any underwear. In the heat of the moment she had forgotten to pay attention to this critical detail and now she could not recall how much she had peeled off his body.

The stove door opened and shut, and she heard Cody head back outside, presumably for more firewood. She decided there was no time like the present for some snooping. She pulled on her T-shirt and pants and scooted back into the bedroom. An eighteenth century mahogany dresser rested in the far corner, to the left of the sliding glass doors opening onto the deck. Madeleine pulled open a top drawer and found it full of socks, all folded in half and stacked with no space left. She opened another drawer and found under shirts, stacked with one-inch cedar balls rolling between the stacks.

"Lookin' for something?"

Madeleine swiveled around and bumped the drawer shut with her fanny. She gripped the edge of the dresser behind her and tried to look nonchalant.

"A sweater," she answered. "Do you have a sweater I could wear? All I could find was socks and undershirts."

"In the closet on the shelf, left side." He eyed her with only the barest hint of a smile. "Ya couldda asked."

"Right. Well, I didn't want to bother you," replied Madeleine. She stepped around a low arm chair and opened the closet. The shelf was stacked with Ziplock bags of sweaters. She pulled one down and removed a navy hooded sweatshirt emblazoned with a Georgetown University logo. She held it against her body and stretched out the arm.

"Looks like it was made for you," Cody commented.

"Men's extra-large usually gives me just enough room in the bust."

"I'm surprised you didn' just get a flannel shirt outa the closet. You seem like the flannel type to me."

"And you don't seem like the commando type to me," she said, cutting to the chase. "You're too much of a neatnik. Were you ever in the military?"

"Ya forgot to shut the door." The carrier nodded his head toward the closet.

"See what I mean?" Madeleine pulled the sweatshirt over her head. "Who cares if the door is open for two minutes?" she mumbled through the cotton.

"I do. Shut the door."

CHAPTER 30

The ride back to town was uneventful. Madeleine sulked much of the way and Cody kept his own counsel. As they rounded the corner onto Rio Road, a familiar white sedan moved in behind them.

"I hope they been keeping an eye on the house while we been gone,' said Cody.

"Why?" asked Madeleine. "Does Cosmo need witness protection?"

"Something like that," he replied. "I booby-trapped the house."

"Do what?"

"Somebody thinks we're on to him. That's what the B&E was about and that's why the guy got into Betty with you." Cody pulled off his Red Sox hat and ran long fingers through his curls. He shook his head and replaced the cap. "It's a matter o' time before he figures out where ya went. You needa think about who ya been talkin' to and what they know. Who did you talk spook shit to?"

"You mean the Suits?" She stared through the glass as they crossed the fast food alley of Emmett Street. The strip was lit but businesses were dark and traffic was light. "Nobody. Well, maybe Rita, but mostly I told her I was learning surveillance with you." Madeleine checked herself. "I did say something about working with the police to break up a burglary ring, but it was a joke. Do you think she took me seriously?"

"Somebody did. Think about who Rita's friends are."

"Yeah. So many drugs, so little time. She hasn't acted like she was doing coke for a while, but she's definitely been borrowing from the drawer. We had a chat about that. That's actually how I got her to switch around and take some extra shifts so I could run the route with you."

Cody laughed. "Blackmail? I like it. Maybe we should go into business together an' start our own syndicate. You can be the muscle."

"That's right," said the laundress. "Never turn your back on the lady with the knife."

"You know, Mad, you got the perfect place to launder the money and Winnie is the perfect cover. Nobody would ever suspect the Church Lady."

"Very funny," said Madeleine, unamused. She thought about how easy it had been to turn a bad situation with Rita to her own advantage "Is this how people become corrupt?"

"Nah," said the carrier. "Maybe a few, but ya gotta have larceny in yer soul somewhere." He reached over and squeezed Madeleine's thigh.

"What you did with Rita was get back what she took. You weren't going after her just to watch her squirm. If ya fired her and took her to court to get it back, you'd spend more on lawyers than you'd win. This way there's no fuss, no muss. You done good." The guttural o's rolled off his tongue.

The Datsun cruised past the vocational school and into the S turns. They crossed a creek and headed back up toward the oldest section of Charlottesville. The houses were older, larger buildings, of brick or frame construction, often surrounded by one or two acre lots and bounded by wrought iron fences.

Madeleine's spirits lifted. Cody's hand rested on her thigh, leaving her warm in every way. If he held a grudge over her snooping, he didn't show it. His face was serene in the slight glow from the dash. He signaled and turned left at the light by the courthouse. The carrier glanced at her face and spread his fingers across her knee.

"Whatcha thinkin'?" he asked.

"You are so different from Jerry," she answered.

"God, I hope so." Cody made a face.

"Jerry nursed a grudge like a Rottweiler nurses pups. He wouldn't ever tell me anything, and if he caught me trying to find out on my own, I'd hear about it until the end of time. Every argument was another opportunity to haul out something I did ten years ago."

"That takes too much energy," said Cody. "If ya wanna know something, ask. If it's none of yer business, I'll say so. I don't lie. I don't cheat. And I do believe you are more than enough for one man."

The carrier made another turn and came up the back way to his father's house. At a discreet distance, the white sedan also rounded the corner and pulled over to the curb.

"Wait here. This won't take a minute," he told Madeleine.

The laundress sighed and watched as he walked back to the sedan and spoke to its occupants. A couple minutes later he bounded the concrete steps and entered the gray frame house. She watched the windows for signs of movement, but saw neither movement nor light of any kind. When Cody returned she peppered him with questions.

"What took you so long? Is Cosmo all right? How come you were working in the dark? Oh, wait . . . do you have black-out curtains?"

The carrier's hand shot up, fending off the verbal assault. "Down girl! No more java for you," he said. He stowed his newspaper gear under the seat. "I hadda check and re-set the booby-trap; then I fed the cat. Cosmo's fine but he's bored. I hadda make sure he couldn't set off the trap. And yeah, those are black-out curtains. Remember my dad, the vampire?"

"Right, with the coffin in the basement. I'm looking next time I go in there," said Madeleine. "Is it soundproof as well?"

"Not as much as I'd like," Cody replied. "I betcha we could create some hellacious sound effects to test it out. Stakeout probably needs some help stayin' awake."

"Yeah, that'll really look good to Detective Knight. He already thinks I murdered Jerry and tried to murder the sweatshirt guy. Now he'll have a motive for it."

"How does sleepin' with me give you a motive to kill the sweatshirt guy?"

"Maybe I hired the guy to rough up Jerry and scare him into leaving. It went wrong and Jerry died. I got pissed off and attacked him. Anyway, that's what the detective said, except he's guessing I'm sleeping with the sweatshirt guy." She shuddered. "The very thought of it gives me the creeps."

"No shit," said Cody. He started the engine and pulled a U-turn. They waved at the stake-out as they passed and headed through the Park Street neighborhood toward Rio Road.

"Can we make a detour before we get the papers rolled?" asked Madeleine. "I need some different clothes."

"Bustin' outa my sweater?"

"You wish. I need a change of scenery. Except for the play, I've been wearing the same two T-shirts and jeans for the past five days. It's getting old," replied the laundress.

"Darn," said Cody. "I was hopin' you wanted to break out the flimsy negligées."

"Get real. Do I look like the sexy negligée type?"

"Mae West had a body like yours and she was one

of the hottest sex symbols of her era." He gave her an approving glance and squeezed her thigh.

"'Come up and see me sometime,'" said Madeleine in a sultry tone.

"Exactly," said the carrier.

Ten minutes later Cody pulled up in front of Madeleine's white frame house. He followed Madeleine under the car port past stacked cases of empty Old Milwaukee bottles, through the door into the kitchen. The two of them stood transfixed in the center of the room. It was totally devoid of appliances, kitchen table and chairs, spice rack and canisters. A hand full of dust bunnies rolled over three pennies and the twist-off cap to a beer bottle in the space that the stove and refrigerator had once occupied. The red-trimmed art deco clock was missing from the wooden valence above the kitchen sink and window, and the ancient red-framed guide to the use of spices in cooking no longer graced the opposite wall. In their stead were two conspicuously white patches, one six-inch round, one twelve-by-eighteen inch rectangular, in stark contrast to the rest of the yellowed paint of the rest of the kitchen.

"What happened here?" asked the carrier. "Stay here."

Madeleine surveyed the room in silence and then followed him into the living room. Every stick of furniture except the recliner and sofa was gone. The built-in shelves no longer held knickknacks, books or VCR tapes; the walls held neither posters, nor pictures nor art of any kind.

On the floor in front of the mantle was the picture of Madeleine's softball team. She picked it up and set it on the mantle.

"Janey," she said. Her hoarse voice echoed across the room. "She had Jerry's key."

"Mad, I don't think even Janey would do this." He put his arm around her shoulders.

"You don't get it. Janey hates my guts and she

probably thinks I'm the reason her brother is dead. This is retribution," said Madeleine. She pointed at the couch and recliner, standing solitary against the wall. "The only reason she wouldn't take these was because they smelled like a bar. She wouldn't sit on either one."

"Well, let's see what else is left," said Cody and he headed up the stairs.

The upstairs rooms were equally well cleaned out, though most of the personal items in the bathroom remained untouched. Madeleine ran her hand across the lids of lotions and perfumes on the vanity. The bottle of J. Worth "Je Reviens" perfume was gone, leaving a nice clean rectangle where it had sat, unopened, for six years. The perfume had belonged to her mother and the scent around the cap alone was sufficient to bring warm memories of her embrace.

Madeleine turned her mind and body away and headed for the bedroom. It was bare. She opened her bedroom closet and found nothing but two pairs of red rubber-toed sneakers.

"Unbelievable," she said aloud. "Why the hell didn't she take the shoes? Do they stink?"

She shut the door and went looking for Cody. He wasn't upstairs. She went downstairs, her footsteps resounding from the stair treads. She opened the front door and found him on the street talking to their escort in the white sedan. The two men got out of the vehicle and approached the house.

"Ma'am, we'll need you to stay here until the back-up arrives. You can sit in our car while you wait."

CHAPTER 31

"And so, Ms. Dreiser, we meet again," said Detective Knight as he took a seat in the interview room and laid his notebook on the table. "It looks like your boyfriend cleaned your house for you."

"Not funny. It was Janey, Jerry's sister. I don't know what she did with the stuff, but she's the one who did it. I know it." Madeleine crossed her arms over her bosom.

"Exactly how do you know it?" asked the detective.

"It's the only thing that makes sense. Jerry's dead. Janey thinks I'm the reason and she's making me pay for it. She probably started out thinking she'd take what was his, and then just kept on going. Did you notice what she left?" asked the laundress.

"Bathroom toiletries, a couch and recliner," answered the detective without looking at his notes.

"And my sneakers. She left two pairs of sneakers in the closet. She took all the clothes and left those shoes. I don't know why she'd take the clothes. She's a skinny little witch; it's not as if she could wear them."

"There was an item missing from your bathroom, Ms. Dreiser. What was that?" asked Detective Knight. He picked up his notebook and pulled a pen from his jacket pocket.

Madeleine's foot began to twitch. She crossed her legs and stretched them out under the table.

"A bottle of perfume," she replied.

"What brand of perfume was it?" he asked, pen poised to write.

"Why are you so interested in a bottle of perfume?"

"How do I know that it actually *was* perfume? Maybe that was your dope stash," said the detective,

141

tapping the notebook with his pen.

"It was J. Worth, 'Je Reviens,' from France. It was my mother's. Now are you satisfied?"

"I might be satisfied when I have your sweatshirt friend in custody and can review all this with him in person. Right now all I have is your statements, an assault, two burglaries, two matching blood samples, and a body.

"Very well," he said, closing the notebook. "You have a route to do. You can go. Do not, I repeat, do not leave town. If anything else occurs to you that may be relevant, call me. You have my number." He pocketed the pen and stood up.

Madeleine followed the detective back to the front entrance where Cody was chatting with the officer who had stopped them during her first night on the route. The officer nodded his head hello and she nodded back.

"Cody, I'm disappointed but not surprised. You ducked my team and left town with my witness," said Detective Knight.

"Aw, come on, Detective. It's not like I went to Maui," Cody replied. "It's not safe here. One look at her place oughtta tell ya that, and I'm not too sure about my dad's place either. You know where I went. Tell Willie to put a deputy out there. They got nothin' better to do except raid pot patches and run domestics. I'm sure somebody'd be happy to get outa doing that."

"I'll take the matter into consideration. In the meantime, she stays here in Albemarle. Got it?" Detective Knight looked Cody in the eye.

"Got it," said the carrier. "Can we go? I'm runnin' extra papers tonight."

"Go. Just stay out of trouble so I can get some

sleep." The detective rolled his head slightly to the left and something cracked in his neck. "Finally," he said, and walked out.

Cody turned to the other officer. "Rick, where's the game this week?"

"Jay's house. You in?"

"Yeah," replied the carrier. "I'll see ya there." He pushed the door open and followed Madeleine out.

"What was that about? Do you play poker with the cops? Are you some kind of cop? They don't treat you like everybody else. What was that business about 'my witness?' I thought I was a suspect. Does this mean I'm not a suspect anymore?"

"Breathe, woman! Anybody ever tell you ya learn a whole lot more with your mouth shut?" He leaned into her ear, "Not to mention, not everybody has to hear what you *don't* know."

Madeleine stared at her feet in shame. She was blowing it, the same way she blew everything else in her life. Open mouth, insert foot, shove it all the way to the hip. She walked through the parking lot to her car in silence. As Cody reached to unlock the Datsun, she took the keys from his hand.

"That's okay. I'll drive." She opened the passenger door for him. He got in and reached across to unlock the driver's side for her. She slid into the seat and shut the door. "I'll drive. You talk."

"Okay," said Cody. "Every Tuesday night there's a game at somebody's house. Potter and I share game night at his house. I got in on the game through him and none o' the rest wanna go out to Greene. Lucky me.

"I am not a cop. Some of the older ones know my dad, so they cut me a little more slack than they do most carriers. I don't want any interference, so I let 'em know if I see anything they might be interested in . . . anything what looks like a drunk driver, a B&E or an assault. I don't fool with the drug stuff. That's a whole other kinda ball game."

"What about Rita and the crystal?" asked Madeleine. She started the engine, stretched her arm behind Cody's head and looked over her shoulder before pulling out of the space.

"That's personal. Rita is messing around on your turf," said Cody. He removed his Red Sox cap, turned it backwards and shoved it down over his curls.

"As far as the 'witness' versus 'suspect' distinction goes, technically you're a witness. I think you'll also be on the suspect list until we figure out who the sweatshirt guy is."

"We?" asked Madeleine. Her heart began to race.

"Yeah, you and me," Cody answered, his lips spreading into a wide grin. The hunt was on.

CHAPTER 32

The bundles stacked up all the way to the ceiling of the Datsun's rear hatch and halfway up the back seat. There was a stack of bundles for Winnie's route set aside on the dock in its usual place.

"How are we going to get all this in, let alone delivered?" Madeleine asked, staring at the mountain of newsprint in her car.

"We'll get it done," Cody replied. "I do this all the time. It's all in how you organize it. We'll come back for Winnie's." He ignored Winnie's stack but counted all the rest of the bundles. The carrier pulled a sheaf of print-outs from his back pocket and opened the driver's door. "Let's roll."

They pulled into the IHOP lot and Cody retrieved the bundle from the back seat. He reached across the stacks and locked the rear door behind Madeleine.

"Lock your door," he instructed her.

"But you'll be right—" Madeleine protested.

"Do it," said Cody. He zipped up his navy windbreaker, locked both left doors and headed for the newspaper stand.

Madeleine pushed the lock in and sighed. It wasn't that she disagreed with Cody; she just didn't like being bossed. She imagined Janey, in league with the sweatshirt guy, pawing through her belongings. Sweatshirt guy didn't need to come after her again. Surely he had already done enough damage to her. Her foot began to tap.

"Enough!" she said and turned to the back seat for papers to roll.

The dash was set up and a strap of bags dangled from the mirror. Madeleine reached under the driver's seat for the bag of rubber bands. There was an envelope under the bag. She pulled it out and held it to catch the street light. The utility bill from Virginia Power was addressed to Cody, but the address was his father's address. She tucked it back under the seat, strung a handful of rubber bands on the gear shift, and replaced the bag on top of the envelope.

Madeleine had never really thought about where Cody lived. He never said and she had no reason to ask. She searched her memory for references and could only come up with a few, none of which specified an address. What was it he said about keeping her at his house, something about making it an easy job for the stake-out? She wondered if the bungalow in Greene County was his home. That would explain it being easy for the stake-out: they could let the Greene County police follow the pair and radio the point where they would cross back into Albemarle.

But why not say that it was his house? Why did Cody say "we have a place in Greene" instead of "I?" Why call the Charlottesville house his dad's house when the utilities were in Cody's name? How could he afford to keep two places on a carrier's earnings? No one except the executives in the newspaper industry makes much money, and carriers make the least.

It didn't sit well. What else was he keeping from her? Once again there was that hole where information ought to be.

There was a rap on the window. Madeleine's heart stopped and she dropped the paper she was banding.

"Boy, you were off in Never-Never Land. I understand now how ya didn't notice the sweatshirt guy 'til you were all the way into Betty," said Cody as she unlocked the door. He marked down his returns on the print-out and tucked it over the visor.

"Fayed had a good laugh about the Suits bein' theater people. I think he's still gonna get security cams though. He was clearing shelf space for a split screen monitor." The carrier chuckled and pulled a couple of bundles from the back seat.

"I see you been busy. That's good. We'll get through faster, maybe even have time to get a mocha later."

"Maybe we should put the stake-out to work rolling papers," Madeleine suggested. "What else do they have to do?"

"What?! Take their time away from eating donuts? Perish the thought!" said Cody.

He was in such a jovial mood that the laundress didn't want to spoil things, but there was that niggly little detail of a home place. She tried to think of an innocent way to broach the subject. There wasn't one.

"Looks like I'll be sorting through the 'lost and found' for clothes for a while,' she said. She bagged a paper and dropped it into the pile between her feet. "I'll check Good Will and The Army for furniture."

"Why not buy it new? Won't your homeowners' insurance cover it?"

"I think I'm covered if the house burns down, but I didn't sign up for theft coverage. It never occurred to me that anyone would want what I had. I guess Janey must figure I have insurance too."

"Doll, you can stay with me 'til you get set up again." Cody twirled a bagged paper and tied it off. It landed with a plop on the stack at her feet.

"Cody, where exactly do you live?" Her hands lay motionless in her lap while her heart hammered away in her chest.

"I been wondering how long it would take you to ask," he said. "I'm glad you asked and didn't go snooping through my stuff to find out."

Madeleine grimaced. "I didn't go snooping. The bill was under the rubber bands in *my* car. It has your dad's address and it's in your name. Do you live there or do you live in Greene?" She rolled up a paper and banded it.

"Yes," he answered.

"Yes which?" She shook the paper at him. "Stop messing with me."

"Yes to both."

"Both?" The laundress was confused.

"'Oh, how can you be in two places at once when you're not anywhere at all,'" Cody sang an imitation of Firesign Theatre. He rolled a paper, banded and slid it into a bag.

"Doll, you could figure this out but you don't wanna to see it. Remember I told you my dad used to be with the OSS? He never retired. The agency was dissolved but the players just moved into other branches of the State Department until they formed a new agency. They still had all the files intact, stowed away in a warehouse until they got funding."

"Your father is a spy?" Somehow she hadn't translated 'working with the OSS' into modern day espionage.

"Dad works for the State Department. It's not important which agency. If you asked him, he'd tell you he's an accountant for the government. He's based in northern Virginia and comes home for R&R. Everything's in my name. It's safer that way."

"Why does an accountant need to worry about being safe?" Madeleine rolled a paper and banded it. She tapped it on her knee twice and then smacked Cody's knee. "Black ops! He tracks funding for black ops!"

"Keep your voice down. Nobody who works for any of these agencies ever says exactly what they do and ya don't ask. If yer payin' attention, ya notice that about six months after somebody comes back from a trip to Korea or Bosnia or the Middle East, things suddenly heat up there. I know other guys whose folks work for one or another agency, an' they say the same thing.

Mom once said he called her during the Cuban

Missile Crisis an' told her to have boxes of canned food, bottled water an' other stuff packed by the door. No other instructions, just wait an' be ready to fly. When he showed up it was weeks later an' he wouldn't talk about it. Wouldn't talk about anything, just sat there silent for almost a month."

"Sounds like the stories you hear about Vietnam vets," said Madeleine.

"Yeah, except he didn't see combat. If he did, he couldn't talk about it anyway. Mom respected that, but I don't know how she lived with all that silence. Ya gotta love someone a whole lot to do that."

"Maybe it's like living with an alcoholic," Madeleine said. "At first you think it's an isolated thing. Then you think it doesn't happen very often, so no biggie. Don't rock the boat. By the time you realize it's a problem, that elephant in the living room is too big to move."

"Speaking of too big to move, maybe we should unload some o' these babies before you're buried up to your eyeballs," said the carrier. "With any luck we'll just miss Pepe."

They rushed through the Carrsbrook, Greenbrier and Four Seasons subdivisions, stopped at the Fashion Square Mall to roll more papers, and headed south to drop Ellen's bundles. Madeleine's shoulder, wrist and hands ached from the repetitive motions of bagging and tossing. Her bladder was also full. Madeleine tried crossing her legs but there were too many papers to move.

"Cody, can we take a pee break? We're close to the laundromat. It'll only take me a minute."

Cody stretched his wrist out from the windbreaker and looked at his watch. The phosphorescent dial read four-twelve. "Okay. How about I drop you off, drop the bundles and meet you in ten minutes? That enough time?"

"Uh huh," she said, barely listening. She pulled the key off the ring.

"If you get done faster, radio me and I'll swing back

around." The carrier pulled up to the building. He reached into the area behind his seat, pulled out an orange walkie-talkie and handed it to her.

Madeleine hooked the radio to her belt and turned it on. She jumped out of the car, praying that the key would turn in the old lock without hanging up.

The lock turned easily and the laundress ran into the restroom, unzipping as she ran. Moments later she emerged feeling the weight of the world lift from her shoulders. She still had a few minutes before Cody would return, so she opened the door to the utility room to see if she could locate Cody's handiwork.

The cameras were well hidden. Madeleine didn't see anything that even remotely looked like one. What she did see was her full mop bucket, with the mop still in it, standing like a sentry at the back door. She rolled it over to the sink, wrang out the mop and removed both wringer and mop.

A car pulled up on the street to the side of the building and she heard footsteps on the pavement. Cody was quicker than she planned. He would not be happy to find her looking for cameras. She rehearsed her excuse mentally as the door opened up front. Damn, it was time to haul out the other excuse too, the one about why the door was unlocked. Mop in hand, she marched out front.

"You gave me the bum's rush so fast I forgot to dump—" The words died in her throat.

"Lookin' for your honey?" asked the man in the gray hooded sweatshirt. "He and the G-men are busy at the moment. I don't think he'll be back for a while." He blocked the space between Madeleine and the front door. She darted toward the other end of the counter, but he shifted his stance to block that as well.

"Let's you and me get re-acquainted. We have some unfinished business. Rock, paper, scissors. Last time you had the sharp; this time I do."

He drew a switch blade from his sweatshirt pocket

and released the catch. The blade swung out and he lunged for the laundress.

"No!" shouted Madeleine. She turned the mop handle sideways between both hands and blocked the knife. The man began to advance toward her, wagging the blade to get an angle into her. The laundress backed up and took the handle like a bat with both hands. In a flash she swung from the left and knocked the knife from his hand. It clattered to the floor by the dryer, too far for either to reach.

On her belt the orange walkie-talkie began to chirp, "Break fourteen for Mad Elaine. Break fourteen for Mad Elaine. Earth to Mad. Earth to Mad. Come in." She ignored it.

"I really want to do this with my bare hands anyway," he grunted as he tried to wrest the mop from her hands.

Madeleine kicked at his injured left leg, but lost her balance as he pushed forward on the handle. She fell backward through the doorway to the utility room, tripping on the wringer and slamming into the rear end of the dryers.

"Oh, this is gonna be good," he said, moving in on her.

The draft through the open doorway brought a familiar scent to Madeleine's nostrils—"Je Reviens". Her eyes opened wide.

Clinging to the mop handle with both hands, the laundress sucked in air and pushed off from the dryer. She heaved upward as hard as she could toward the shelf over the sink and then released the handle. Sweatshirt Man stepped into the wringer and lurched forward onto the floor. The handle smacked the bleach bottle, sending the bottle hurtling into the bucket. A cloud of yellowish green gas rose from the bucket. The man coughed and writhed as the acrid gas seared his windpipe.

"Bob! Hurry up! Did you find it?" called a woman's voice from the counter.

Cardboard boxes flew as Madeleine forced open the slide bolt on the back door. The man on the floor made a feeble gasp and his hand groped at her heel. The laundress launched her shoulder against the door and it gave way. Precious cold air enveloped her as her lungs exploded. She collapsed into the grass, mindless of the pre-dawn frost or the stars overhead.

"Mad?" A warm hand touched her cheek.

"Grmpf," she mumbled, but made no effort to move. "Took you long enough."

"Guess you were right about the bleach. Two for the price o' one."

"Two?" Madeleine opened an eye. "Dang!"

"Yup," said Cody. "Good job."

Blue lights came flashing around the corner, followed by red lights. Cody helped Madeleine up and together they sat on the curb while Detective Knight's team cordoned off the area with yellow tape and inspected the carnage. Madeleine took the proffered rescue squad blanket but refused to let them check her lungs. There was only one set of hands she wanted touching her.

"Did you hear the radio?" asked Cody.

"Uh huh," answered the laundress. "I couldn't answer. I was indisposed.

"I don't suppose the Detective will believe it was self-defense." She drew her knees to her bosom and wrapped the blanket tighter.

"He'll believe it when he sees it. It's all on tape." He took his hat off, ran a hand through the curls and replaced the hat, bill forward.

"Well, not the part where Sweatshirt Man pulled out the switchblade and waggled it at me." She stretched her neck to get clear of hair obstructing her view.

"Nah." He grinned. "There's a camera in one o' the flower pots."

"Aren't you slick," she said, remembering his diligence in watering her plants.

"How didja get it away from him?" asked the carrier. He pulled the hair away from the blanket and tucked it behind her ear.

"Softball comes in handy. Turns out I'm a right handed pitcher, but I bat lefty."

"A woman after my own heart," said Cody.

CHAPTER 33

The sun was peeping up over Rio Hill as the Datsun rolled into parking lot at the Charlottesville Daily Progress. Potter and the old geezer were swapping stories as they dumped their returns. Madeleine lowered the back on her seat to almost horizontal and shut her eyes. Bits of the conversation between the carriers drifted into hearing but she was past caring.

"Do what?! Bob and Ellen? How the hell did they have time to do it? They were running a route," said the old geezer. He pulled a round tin from his pocket and tucked some tobacco into his lower lip.

"They had plenty o' time to scout out the neighborhoods. Didn't ya think it was weird that none of the houses were Progress customers? Every one either subscribed to the Observer or didn't get a paper."

"All this time we've been calling them 'B&E' and they've been living up to the title. What did they do with the loot?" asked Potter.

"Fenced it in D.C. is my guess," replied Cody. "There aren't enough pawn shops and flea markets 'round here to absorb all that."

"That makes it a federal case. You're going to have FBI knocking at your door," said Potter.

"Tell me about it. And, to top it off, they're the two people who died at Mad's laundromat from the chlorine gas this morning. Bob was the guy in the sweatshirt—"

"What guy in the sweatshirt? You lost me back there with the chlorine gas, bud," said the old geezer. He turned and spat.

"That's cuz you don't read the paper, Pop," said Cody. "Remember a few days ago when some fella tried to assault Mad at the IHOP? The same one broke into her house that night and he came after her again tonight at the laundromat. That was Bob."

"Well, what was he after? That's a hell of way to scout up a new girlfriend."

"Police think it was drugs," said Cody.

"Yeah, that's what they always think," said Potter, "but maybe he was tired of three hundred pounds worth of Ellen. And you know that woman took some maintenance—always crabby."

"Ever wonder if she threw Bob around like she did the bundles?" The old man turned his head and spat.

"Yeah. Remember the time . . ."

Cody heard his cue and tipped his hat goodbye. Madeleine was sound asleep on her left side in the front seat, knees drawn up and red rubber toes curled around the gear shift. Cody pulled the orange walkie-talkie from her belt.

"Fat lotta good *you* did," he said to the radio, and stowed it under the seat.

"You talking to me, mister?" asked a sleepy voice beside him.

"Nah. Go back to sleep, doll," replied the carrier. He lowered the brake and put the car into reverse.

"Cody?"

"Yeah?"

"I think Mom was in there with me."

"How come?"

"I could smell her."

"You could smell her?"

"Uh huh. Maybe she was there because she thought I might die or maybe it was to help me in some way."

"Didja tell Knight whatcha smelled?"

"No. He wouldn't understand." She rolled onto her back and brought the seat back to upright position.

"Actually. I think he would," said Cody. He pulled

the radio back out and turned it on.

"Break Fourteen for Circ Man, come in" he said into the microphone.

"Circ Man here. Go ahead," the radio chirped.

"Can ya patch me over to Knight's office?"

"Roger. I'll get back to you. Over," said the circulation manager. A moment later the radio chirped again.

"Hey Detective, I think I got a lead for ya," said Cody. "I think you'll find the missin' perfume at B&E's place. See if it ain't what she's wearing. Dinner at Duner's is on me if I'm wrong. Over."

"We'll check it out," said a scratchy voice on the other end. "Duner's, huh. I'll hold you to that. You're on record. Over and out."

Cody tucked the walkie-talkie under the seat. He steered the car through the S-turns on Park Street and back up the hill toward home.

"So you think Ellen took Mom's perfume?" asked the laundress. "I guess I was being silly." Her red rubber toes tapped each other under the dash.

"Nah, Mad. You weren't silly. You didn't have time to put it all together, and I could be all wet."

"You could be buying the Detective the most expensive dinner of his life if you're wrong," said Madeleine.

"Doll, if I'm wrong, I'll buy you *both* dinner at Duner's." He squeezed her thigh. "By the way, didja notice we don't have an escort anymore?"

Madeleine stared at the rear view mirror for a minute. "Does this mean I'm not a suspect anymore?"

"I think so. And I think the Detective was real impressed with you."

"For what?" Madeleine was skeptical.

"For thinkin' so quick on your feet. The first time he chalked up to a lovers' spat. The second time he had other evidence against that."

"What other evidence—the video from the store?"

"Oh, much better'n that," said Cody. "You'll see."

"Who's going to take over that other route now that Sweatshirt Man is gone?" asked Madeleine. "You can't do all the routes. We'd still be out there if Potter hadn't done some of yours."

"I guess Circ Man will divvy it up unless he's got someone lookin' for a route. There's always an ad in the classifieds. There's a lot o' turnover in this business. Remember what Pop said to you the second night about carriers lasting about three months? It's true. We don't get vacations and it's a seven day a week job unless you work out something with a friend. Most people don't like that."

"Why do you do it?" asked Madeleine.

"I'm sockin' it away so I can retire early. I wanna travel and there aren't many jobs where you can take off for a month whenever you want."

"Your dad seems to travel a lot. It seems like he's gone more than he's home."

"True, but consider what he does. It's a job with a lotta risk. He's not out there for fun." Cody turned into the alley behind the house and parked at the edge of the yard.

"I feel like we're sneaking in after a date," said Madeleine as she followed him onto the back porch. Cody smiled but said nothing.

The kitchen was dark except for a wedge of light from the living room. A man lay stretched out on the couch under the throw and on the opposing side of the coffee table sat a woman, roped to a chair and gagged with a neck tie. Cody flipped on a light switch as they passed from the dining room into the living room.

"Rita?" asked Madeleine, dumfounded.

The gag prevented anything coherent from escaping Rita's lips, but anger flashed in her eyes. Strands of tawny hair stuck out from the gag, and her nostrils flared at the base of her reddish beak.

"Ah, the prodigal son returns," said the man on the

couch. He peeled off the blanket and stood up. With the exception of the eyes that blazed blue, there was little resemblance between father and son. The elder Cody was slightly shorter than Madeleine, had a stocky build and ruddy complexion.

"More like the prodigal dad," said Cody. "Dad, this is Madeleine."

"Pleased to meet you, sir," said Madeleine and extended her hand.

"Warren Cody. The pleasure is all mine." Wavy silver hair fell across his face as he kissed the top of her hand. "Rarely do I come home to find half of my work done for me. At this point I am merely awaiting transport back to Quantico for this young lady, whom I found languishing in a crude but very effective burglar deterrent."

"Cut the crap, Dad. Is Knight done with her?"

"Detective Knight was otherwise engaged. Something about two people in a laundromat with mustard gas." The elder Cody flicked his wrist and straightened the inside sleeve of his jacket. "The Bureau will take it from here. You know how they do hate to share.

"Have we any coffee in the house?" asked Warren.

"No."

"Yes." They answered in unison.

"It's late, Dad," said Cody.

"I think there's an unopened pound in the freezer. I can brew some up in no time," said Madeleine, undeterred.

"You have to work today. You need to sleep."

"No, I don't. The only thing I need to do is call people to tell them they get their clothes tomorrow. I don't even need to do that. I can give the list to Winnie. If the theater people are leaving, I can always drive it up to DC. What's another hundred miles? I do that every night." She pushed flyaway hair behind her ears.

"William Joseph Donovan Cody, I have had enough of you railroading me. I'm tired of guessing about who or what you are. I want to know what the hell is going on. I'm

going to make a pot of coffee. You guys can figure it out."
The laundress turned on her heel and marched toward the
kitchen.

Scuffling noise, followed by a loud bump, sounded
behind her. Rita was on her back on the floor, still tied to
the chair. Cody picked her up and tightened the knots. He
unplugged the telephone and stuffed it into the pocket of
his windbreaker.

"By the way, Rita," said Madeleine from the kitchen
doorway, "you're fired."

The door swung back and forth behind her. Cody
looked at his father.

"See what I mean?"

"I do," replied the older man. "—very much alike."

Cody brought dining room chairs into the kitchen and they
sipped steaming aged Sumatra, three cow hands around the
fire. Cody tipped his chair back on two legs and set his cup
on the counter. He nodded toward the door to the dining
room. Warren reached behind himself and pushed the door
closed.

"So, Dad, how does all this local mayhem fit into
your caseload?"

"The Bureau has been investigating a string of
burglaries up and down the eastern seaboard," said Warren.
"It appears that the burglaries are done by locals, the stolen
items are fed by truck to a warehouse and from there into a
network of pawn shops and flea markets. The same
network transfers drugs back to localities."

"You mean it's like when the Fed Ex guy brings you
papers to sign? You sign them, put them into a pre-paid
envelope, and send them back with him. That's like regular
business." Madeleine got up and poured another cup of
coffee.

"Exactly," said Warren. "It's very organized crime.

Obviously we're more interested in the higher ups, but it helps to find a way into the network. Now that we know that one avenue was a newspaper carrier, we can check out the other strings and see if they show a similar pattern.'

"So any overnight delivery system would do," said Madeleine, stirring in the sugar and cream. She felt liquid flowing through her veins, her fingertips pulsating with the rhythm of her heart. The same energy was traveling through her legs and her foot began to twitch.

"Yeah," Cody agreed. "Could be restaurant supply, grocery or general merchandise trucks in an urban area. Bob had a retired U-Haul truck. He repainted it and painted 'Haul It Away' in the same kinda lettering over the old logo. He sometimes used it on the route, so nobody wouldda noticed anything unusual."

"Something bothers me about the woman who came in the laundromat after the Sweatshirt Guy," said the laundress. "She shouted something to him from the front, but he was thrashing and making all this noise. It was all I could do to get out of there and not breathe that gas."

"Shut yer eyes," Cody instructed her. "Now go back to where ya smelled your mom's perfume. What's the next thing that happened?"

Madeleine winced. "The guy was leaning in on me. I pushed him back and aimed the mop at the bleach bottle. He tripped on the wringer at the same time the bleach went into the bucket."

"What do you hear?" asked Warren.

"A lot of pounding in my ears," said Madeleine. "'Did you find it?' She asked if he found it but I don't know what 'it' was."

"Drugs or money. We need to look at the tapes. Did Knight get them yet?"

"Not all of 'em." Cody smiled and pulled a video tape out of the inner lining of his jacket.

"Good," said Warren in a familiar guttural tone.

"On that note, fellows, I'm going to bed," said Madeleine. She drained her cup and set it in the sink.

"I'll be up in a minute," said Cody. He watched the door swing shut after her and turned to Warren.

"She did really well, don't you think?"

"Exceptionally well," replied the elder Cody. "Did you tell her about Babs?"

"A little. I just said it was a fire." Cody picked his hat up from the counter. He tightened the strap on the inside and put the hat on, bill backward.

Warren cocked his head. "What about Cheryl?"

"Nah," said Cody. He plucked the windbreaker from the back of his chair and draped it across his arm. The beige spiral telephone cord bulged from the pocket. He stuffed it back inside.

The older man frowned and leaned forward. A wave of silver hair dropped between his eye brows. "Rebecca?"

"Dad, just leave it alone, okay?" Cody shoved the chair out of the way with his foot as he stood up.

"Son," said Warren, "you have lived all your life with risk. You were born into it and you had little choice about it. You are older now and you have chosen a path with risk. She deserves to know that."

"I like to keep this on a *need*-to-know basis." Cody leaned back against the kitchen sink and crossed his arms. "Mad's mouth gets away from her sometimes. Granted, she didn't tell Knight what we were doing, but there might be something else, something trivial, that would complicate things. Besides that, she likes to take matters into her own hands. Remember the hotel? That could have been really sticky.

"By the way, the electric bill came yesterday," Cody changed the subject. "We need to settle up before you go. That last time you went to Sarajevo I had to cover everything for three months, and that was a stretch." He pulled the folded bill from his back pocket and handed it to Warren.

Warren reached into his inner jacket pocket and produced a pair of silver-framed eye glasses. He set them just above his nostrils and inspected the bill. He looked across the top of the silver frame at his son.

"All you have to do is say the word and Gladys will put you on the payroll. You don't have to live like a damn Spartan. Maybe having a new girl in your life will loosen you up a little." He pulled out his wallet and handed Cody two crisp Ben Franklins.

"I like this one, young man. If I were twenty years younger I'd go for her myself. You make sure you keep her out of bomb's way."

"That's a job in itself," said the carrier. "Knight thought keeping her here would be enough. Scratch that. I think he needs to fire the stake-out too. They should have picked up on Rita; it was totally predictable, but they were too busy watching Mad."

"Obviously you had that one covered," said Warren with a laugh. "She was strung up and dangling by one foot from that bicycle hook when I arrived. Every time she moved, Cosmo attacked the rope or her hair. She thought I was her guardian angel until I secured her to the chair. Perhaps we should have her tested for rabies. She was positively foaming at the mouth—ruined my best silk tie."

"You know, it could have been you, strung up and dangling by one foot. I told you to call me first," said Cody.

"Ah yes, but 'leave a lentil on the lintel,'" said Warren in a sing-song voice.

"Did you find it or just notice it missing?" asked Cody.

"It was not on the lintel and not on the knob, therefore . . ."

"Assume the worst," they said in unison.

CHAPTER 34

"Well that was one hell of a day," said Madeleine. She laid on the bed in Cody's bathrobe and scratched Cosmo behind the ears. The cat lifted his head so she could scratch his chin. The purring was loud and vibrated all the way through her tummy to her back.

"That was one helluva week," said Cody. "Good thing my route don't run like this all the time. It would wear me out." He removed his watch and laid it on the dresser. The carrier sat down on the ottoman and pulled off his boots and socks. He tucked the tops of the socks into the boot tops, leaving the socks dangling.

"Why don't you put them in the hamper?" asked the laundress.

"It lets them air dry and keeps the spiders out of the boots."

He unsnapped the mother-of-pearl snaps on his shirt and slid his arms out of the sleeves. Madeleine's eyes were riveted to his body as he pulled off the white t-shirt and began to unbutton his fly. She grinned ear-to-ear.

"What are you staring at?" asked the carrier.

"Boxers or briefs," answered the laundress. "Drop 'em, partner!"

AFTERWORD

Aaron Sorkin appears in this novel as a character, much as he did in my laundromat in Charlottesville, VA many years ago. He inspired me then and continues to do so. I feel no need to apologize. After all, he is the screen master of brewing fiction from life experience.

Elizabeth Kerr

Want to share this GOOD NEWS with
a loved one or friend?
There are 2 ways to order your copy of

The Spin

by Elizabeth Kerr

1. Order directly from Beirne Bridge Publishing
www.beirnebridge.com

Made in the USA
Columbia, SC
31 July 2017